ALL THE
DIRTY
PARTS

BY THE SAME AUTHOR

NOVELS

The Basic Eight
Watch Your Mouth
Adverbs
Why We Broke Up
We Are Pirates

NOT NOVELS

Girls Standing on Lawns
Hurry Up and Wait
Weather, Weather

AS LEMONY SNICKET

[list available on request]

ALL THE
DIRTY
PARTS
A NOVEL
DANIEL
HANDLER

B L O O M S B U R Y

NEW YORK · LONDON · OXFORD · NEW DELHI · SYDNEY

Bloomsbury USA

An imprint of Bloomsbury Publishing Plc

1385 Broadway	50 Bedford Square
New York	London
NY 10018	WC1B 3DP
USA	UK

www.bloomsbury.com

BLOOMSBURY and the Diana logo are trademarks of Bloomsbury Publishing Plc

First published 2017

© Daniel Handler, 2017

No responsibility for loss caused to any individual or organization acting on or refraining from action as a result of the material in this publication can be accepted by Bloomsbury or the author.

ISBN: HB: 978-1-63286-804-6
ePub: 978-1-63286-806-0

Library of Congress Cataloging-in-Publication Data

Names: Handler, Daniel, author.
Title: All the dirty parts / Daniel Handler.
Description: New York : Bloomsbury USA, 2017.
Identifiers: LCCN 2016046093 | ISBN 9781632868046
(hardcover : alk. paper) | ISBN 9781632868060 (epub)
Subjects: LCSH: Erotic fiction. gsafd
Classification: LCC PS3558.A4636 A79 2017 | DDC 813/.54—dc23
LC record available at https://lccn.loc.gov/2016046093

2 4 6 8 10 9 7 5 3 1

Typeset by Westchester Publishing Services

Printed and bound in the U.S.A. by Berryville Graphics Inc., Berryville, Virginia

To find out more about our authors and books visit www.bloomsbury.com. Here you will find extracts, author interviews, details of forthcoming events and the option to sign up for our newsletters.

—The opening of Rilke's "Third Duino Elegy" is from Gary Miranda's elegant and illuminating translations, published in a highly recommended volume by Tavern Books, and appears courtesy the translator. The author changed one word, with apologies to same.

—Further thanks are due to Lisa Brown, Charlotte Sheedy, Nancy Miller, Susan Rich, Oscar Hijuelos, Michelle Tea, Andrew Sean Greer, Rebecca Stead, Ayelet Waldman, Dana Reinhardt, and some other early readers (hello, girls) who wish to remain anonymous.

—This is a work of fiction.

FOR MY BEAUTIFUL WIFE

ALL THE
DIRTY
PARTS

LET ME PUT it this way: this is how much I think about sex. Draw a number line, with zero is, you never think about sex and ten is, it's all you think about, and while you are drawing the line, I am thinking about sex. Brush up against me in the hall at school, any girl I am thinking of, the way she smells walking behind her up the ugly staircase, trying to keep it together while my whole body rattles like a squirrel in a tin can. To couple up with them, to capture their whole bodies under a blanket with enough light to see the pleasure of what we are doing. Marinated with it, the snap and the sigh of longing to be inside all of her. It's a story that keeps telling itself to me, my own crackling need in this world lit only by girls who might kiss me, like a flower, like a flytrap, the delicious sex we would have if we weren't in the idiotic marathon of going to class. Oh, good. Calculus. This will clear everything up.

· ·

Waking up in the morning, miserable with bad weather. School in front of me, the whole day, like a wall I'm going to bang my head against. Think of the girls, I tell myself, like cookies in the oven to lure me out of bed. Think of how pretty they are. Don't you want to see them, Cole? Come on, brush your teeth.

· ·

Through a rip in a girl's jeans I see a little light fuzz on her knee. And then the next day it's smooth and gone. Naked, shaving her legs. They shave their legs naked, right? Sitting there in jeans and naked in my head. The razor moving up up her legs. Tell us why your grades have suffered.

· ·

Let me put it this way: let's say you had an arm. Let's say it was an arm, instead, that got stiff and stuck out suddenly and unsightly, and calming it down felt amazing. Tell me you would not think, not wonder what the big deal was to ask people if they could just take a minute and take care of that arm for you.

. .

I look around the cafeteria and think, line us all up, from the person who had an orgasm most recently, to who had one the longest time ago. Now line us up again, from happiest to that girl clenching up alone in tears in a furious sweater. It's the same lineup, isn't it?

. .

Wish I could explain, how these things feel like seduction, even though I know they aren't. If you rumple my hair and leave your hand for a minute on my neck. If you sit and put one of your legs up on something even if you're in jeans. If you lick something off your finger. If you put on lipstick. If you rub your own bare arm. If you bend down for any reason to pick something up off the ground. If you talk to me.

. .

—Give me the details.

Alec always says this. My best friend, waiting on the screen when I get home from a date and am back up in my room taking my good shirt off, a pending always request.

—What, like what?

—Like always.

—You want to know what movie we saw?

—Shut up. You know.

—Tell me.

—The dirty parts. The sex is the details I mean.

So that's what I type. There are love stories galore, and we all know them. This isn't that. The story I'm typing is all the dirty parts.

. .

Because I'm on an adventure. I'm not happy ever after with my first girl. You don't see a movie and say, well now I've seen a movie. You see different ones. You try them and keep trying. Because so much of the rest is bullshit nothing. There's friends, laughing on the weekends, nice as they are to be around. Not enough. Your teachers gesture toward the future but they're on the payroll. Cross-country, the coach pushing us further for no reason but sweat and maybe a trophy to get dusty on the bookshelf. The best songs become a thing you're tired of, parents snap at you and the muddle of the rest of it, all of us unable to be everything to each other all the time every day. But this rushing flesh together is something I know. Girl biting my shoulder with two fingers inside her and my thumb smooth-smooth-moving in a quiet pulse, I get this. If it could all move this way, all these bodies I see, looking me in my eye and moving your hand up and down until I come, if we could all come together always like this, we would chase no different joy.

.   .

It doesn't matter how many girls I've slept with. The number doesn't matter, and it doesn't matter that some of them, for months, were more like lovers, a bigger deal, and that some of them, for a night if by *a night* we mean three hours, it was more like a snack. It's not the number that matters. What matters is that, to me, it doesn't feel like enough.

Eleven, is the number.

.   .

It took me forever to figure: she's pressing against me, there's no way she can't feel me hard against her, and she's not pulling away. But she's not saying anything either, she's not rolling back to take something off. We're just *here*, for hours it feels like, this seesaw of wondering, trying not to ruin it, what's going to happen next.

She won't say, *do you want to?* This is something you have to say. I learned, trial and too many errors, the girls, almost all of them all the time, need to be given the idea. They're already thinking about it, but they need the idea *advanced. Let me put it to you this way.*

. .

It sounds pushy, and I know it does. But it's only pushy inside me sometimes. It's not like I'm violent with it. I've never forced a girl. While we were having sex they all, definitely, wanted it to happen.

Afterwards, though, they felt bad about it sometimes.

. .

—Give me the details.

What details can I give another guy? Describing it isn't anything like it is. You can grab your own arm, anything soft. It's not like your hands on her breasts, shirt hiked up quick and bra unclasped off someplace. What could I tell Alec about it?

Everything, it turns out.

· ·

—Hold it like a candy bar.

We are both giggling. She wipes her hand, sweaty, on the sheet and clutches me again.

—Ow. No. Like a candy bar.

—You know, it's not really helpful because I don't go around holding candy bars all the time. Or do this. Show me.

—OK, like—

—*Oh.* OK. This is like a candy bar? OK. And now, what next do I do?

—Now eat it.

I am pulsing, still laughing, close. It will happen quick and surprise her.

· ·

The first time a girl told me to ejaculate on her face, I was fourteen. She looked right at me when she said it.

She wasn't talking to me, though. She was the star of a movie, but those maybe aren't the right words. It's not really a movie. It's six minutes long and the title on the screen is "Brunette Deep Throat Blowjob With Facial." I don't even know if you'd call it a movie, and you wouldn't really call the girl the star. I don't know what you'd call her.

. .

Alec and I send each other what we're watching. I don't know how it started and we never never talk about it. The only thing we do is reply one word if we like it. *Hot.* It's like one of those things that predict what band you'll like. He figured out I like stuff where the girl talks dirty. I figured out he liked two guys and one girl.

Everybody thinks something is hot.

. .

Glasses, pigtails, busty, fat, shaved, browsing and then searching. On their knees looking up at the camera, waiting on the bed while I sit on mine, scrolling for suggestions for further viewing, captioned below. If you came watching this, you might also like two girls getting fucked in a car. Why yes I would.

· ·

Pants around the ankles, I learned this quick—take the ten seconds to not keep them that way. It's one thing to tuck your shirt up out of your way, but pants end up locked around your shoes and you have to Frankenstein-walk someplace with your dick out hard in front of you like a doorknob. She always laughs and then you have to laugh too and pretend that you also are out of the mood for a few minutes. Don't let it happen. I got to taking off my shoes the minute I'm hanging alone with a girl. Ready to go. Just in case.

· ·

It's not like you're even that hot, is what Jeremy says, Alec says it and other guys too, other versions of the same mystified complaint. And you get so much sex, while we all try and fail, and are in the parking lot watching you and the girl grab some chips from the store, on the way to go out into the nighttime and fuck and, what

I'm wondering is, are they all really trying? Or are they just thinking about it, staring alone at a dream that pops into no one else's head. Because this isn't that. You can dream up anything you want, but for actually having sex with actually a girl you have to *move*. You can think, you can *know*, that girls are a mystery, but put it this way: there are things to do, moves you can make. Meet her, talk to her, laugh with her, nuzzle, handhold, walk somewhere, eat something, by now you've kissed a lot. Kiss more, kiss wilder, kiss the neck, collarbone. Rub against, rub with, hands on the bare waist, the back, the breasts. Guide her hands, the first time you come with her, with the gasp and meeting her eyes. Go down on her. Go down on her naked. Go down on her with fingers inside. Go down on her holding her legs open. Keep asking if she likes it, keep asking what else you can do, until she gets the idea and asks you back. You're naked by now. Sit up naked and rest her head in your lap. It feels so good and say so. Come hard. Kiss her right after to say, of course we still kiss, of course we are going to keep doing this. You can do this. Move slow the first five times. Find a way in. Fuck fuck fuck. Buy her a stuffed animal.

. .

—Cole, you're getting a rep.

Sophomore year Kristen tells me this. She is some-times my friend, definitely the reason I'm not flunking Chemistry, fearless with jokes, saying this next to me on a bench after sitting down like it was a professional meeting, a therapy session.

—A rep?

—It's short for reputation.

—Um, thanks for explaining that.

—You are *going after* girls.

—What?

—You heard me, Cole. Too many—

—Too many girlfriends? Is there some allotment? National statistic?

—It's not *girlfriends*, Cole. You *go after* them and people are talking.

—People?

—And you don't treat them like people.

—What?

—The girls. You sleep around.

I look at her. She's not bad looking, although the hair, somebody should intervene. She's part of a small pack of girls I'd never tangle with. Last year at the Holi-day Formal they were standing outside the ballroom and I thought they were protesting it, so fierce were their faces with not having a good time. She is, I'm realizing, a good spy for me, a weather report from rooms I'm not allowed in.

—OK, I'm not a virgin, yeah.

—I'm not talking about sex, Cole. I'm talking about how it's one girl, and then it's another. You're getting a rep.

—OK.

—OK what?

—OK what do you want me to say, Kristen?

I'm on the bench for no reason, the bus having tossed me at school early. But, across the horrible lawn, three girls are practicing a dance something. She can't even see it, right across from us, three delicious girls, and if I went up and told one of them that I liked how she moved—

Kristen is looking at me like I'm a plume of smoke in the kitchen, right before you yell *fire!* —You don't care that people think it's sleazy. You're going to keep up with it.

—What's wrong with going out with girls? Go yell at *girls*, if you think it's wrong. Why does it bother you anyway, it sounds like you're—

I'm smart enough to stop talking but not smart enough, not quick enough.

—You think I'm *jealous?*

We're both laughing now, but only a little bit. —No, but Kristen, why do you *care?*

—You can be infuriating, Cole. I'm trying to *help* you.

She walks off. She's a virgin, I'm realizing. Some guy is going to *go after* her and then she won't wonder if the sex is worth it, because she'll be busy, instead of analyzing me, having sex. But not, for sure, with her hair like that.

· ·

Arya liked to read a lot. We'd go one round and then lie on the floor, her parents' clock ticking, and I'd hand her her book and I'd take one she'd recommended. Finish the chapter, start up with her cheek and neck and ears until she'd sort of sigh and find a bookmark and round two. I read a lot with her, that's one thing. *Ballad of the Sad Café*. Not bad, but she liked it better than me.

· ·

Amelie, she was crazy breathless Jesus Christ beautiful. In the light blue dress stepping out of the mall through a revolving door it was light and miraculous like a moonbeam in a Japanese ghost story video game. Her hair was wispy on the back of her smooth neck, I didn't even want to touch her, it was so beautiful. But, you know, I did.

. .

I taught Alana how to skip rocks, with my hand over her hand with the stone in it, like that. Also on a park bench, dark without wind kicking dirt on us, I taught her to make me come, basically the same way. You're getting the hang of it. You're a natural.

. .

Doze off after, wake up, and Adrienne's mad I was asleep. I'm supposed to, I guess, be staring into her eyes and saying something. But I'm so comfortable with you, is what I tell her instead. She's halfway OK with it. I lean against her and perform a big snore. She's still halfway. I kiss her harder than she thinks will happen right then. She curves one leg over mine. More than halfway now, but I still don't know what I did or how I got out of it.

. .

—Why do you always take your shoes off right when we get inside?

. .

I read their messages too much for clues. *My sister's watching TV,* Amelie sends me, and it means what? She'll be home all night? She's snoopy? Snitching? Doesn't like me?

. .

We fed the ducks together, but they ruined it all, so aggressive it wasn't fun, surrounding us and squawking so loud we just ended up dumping it all on the ground, OK OK, take it, asshole birds. So I get that, if you act too hungry it's not fun anymore. Calm down, sit and wait, you'll get something. But you know, sometimes you're just really really fucking hungry.

. .

Need to find somewhere. My parents are home. Her mom's home. It's cold out. Cars are cramped, and we don't have the car anyway. Dory's having a party, but we can't go upstairs. Fool around a little at the bus stop, in a thing that used to be a payphone. My hands cold. Give up, or try to sneak me through the window. C'mon c'mon. That hotel there, it can't be full, those empty beds no one is using. *Fuck.*

· ·

I say to Kristen, —OK, can I ask you something?
She closes her eyes. —I'm afraid already.
—Stop. Tell me. Uncode it for me.
—It's *de*code, Cole. What?
—OK, if a girl—
—I *knew* it. I'm scared.
—If she says, nothing the first month. Like for the first month we go out, she doesn't want—
—I get it, Cole.
—OK. Which is cool, right? I mean, it's fine.
—A girl making a choice about her own body, yes. That's *cool*, Cole. I'm sooo *glad* you're *fine* with that.
—I *am*. *But*. Second date, we're kissing and she moves my hand to her shirt.

—Ew. Jesus, why are you even—

—OK, but just tell me, decode it, does that mean—

She's trying to cover her eyes and ears at once.

—Shut up shut up shut up—

—Kristen, how am I going to *learn*—

—Shut *up*.

—C'mon.

—You c'mon. Where *were* your hands, anyway, before, in this story, she moved them—

—They were, you know, like on her waist or whatever.

—*Or whatever.* You make me not want to be on Planet Earth, Cole. You force it.

—What?

—Don't *what.* You do. You force it, Cole.

—I don't force people.

—What do you do then?

Now she sounds interested. She is looking at me scientifically, like a professional in her stupid sweater, like I'm the lab animal she might not have to cut open after all. She says it again. —What do you do then?

—Well, like I said. She says nothing for the first month, so nothing's happening.

—But you want it to.

—Yeah, I will admit that. I want it to happen, but

I'm not going to force it to happen, no. I mean, I think we both want it. I think. It feels like it.

—*Aha.*

—What aha? She's the one who moved my hands on her. It happens to her. It happens to both of us.

—*Bullshit.*

She looks around and lowers her voice. —You forced it.

—I helped it along, I guess. I made, I don't know, the space where it could—

—You forced it.

—Stop saying that! What does it mean when she has me touch her? And if I move my hands down? Clamping her legs shut, that means *stop*, that's rapey? Or it means,

—Don't say anything,

—yes right there that spot? If her legs are so tight together that I can't move my legs?

—You could *ask* her, Cole. You could open your mouth.

But our mouths, I can't tell her, are pressed so together then. Kissing the whole time, and then, and it hasn't been a month, her legs just slip open like an exhale.

· ·

—Give me the details.

—I'm not your fucking porn, Alec.

—C'mon c'mon. You love telling me.

I do and I don't, but I tell him. —She held my hand still when I put my finger inside her. Wait, wait, she said, and then I felt it. Her moving around me, like a glove, a shy creature. She moved more. It was like a party trick but it made her come so hard to do it.

—Jesus. That's hot.

—I know.

—I'm hard just hearing about it.

I am too, of course. —Hey don't tell me that, dude. That's private.

· ·

She was the one who taught me how to do it, gently gently running my hands on the sides of her breasts. Thank you, Amelie. I use that on everybody and everybody loves it.

· ·

Moving up her body so my cock is between her breasts and Antoinette half laughs half frowns. —Every guy wants this.

—Well, it's kind of a natural idea.

—I wish I wasn't a C.

—I like them.

—Well, duh.

She's looking out the window now. Her trophies on the windowsill, Antoinette almost made nationals last year. Still straddling her I feel shitty. —But Cole, that's not what they're there for.

· ·

Antoinette liked her nipples really sucked on. Allison liked them almost pinched. Abby, don't touch them. Arya, bite them, but I could never bite them the right way. Always hot, and of course whatever floats the boat, but sometimes, my hand slapped or my ear tugged on, it's, ladies, have a conference and decide. Boys did. We like our cocks sucked, ask anyone.

· ·

—You found it right away.

They always say guys can never find it, that it's hard to find. The clitoris is not hard to find. I mean, it's not like sometimes it's behind her heel or in your desk drawer. Go to where you think it is and root around and you will for sure know when you're right. And porn helps. Find a shaved girl saying "lick my clit" and where he licks, that's the clit. It's educational.

· ·

I'm seventeen now, and no real girl has really told me to ejaculate on her face. Maybe it'll never happen, I told Alec. We've watched a couple blowjobs together, or not together but at the same time, me in my room and he in his, always slightly weird.

—Pornography lied to us.

—I'm writing my congressman.

—OK but let's watch another one first.

· ·

—That guy.

—Yeah.

—I mean, that seriously fucking asshole guy.

I am just around the corner when I hear this. It's Abby talking with a friend of hers who's just brought the news that I'm seeing someone now. They're leaning against the school right where the brick is painted to cover graffiti. I am by the garbage cans, frozen listening. Abby's friend says it again. —Yeah.

—I could fucking kill him,

and part of me wants to round the corner and say, what is it, exactly, that makes me what she says I am? She's the one who said *it just wasn't working out*, and left an envelope in my locker stuffed with little trinkets I bought her. And then some weeks later, yes, I'm with another girl, instead of, what, begging for her to come back outside her window playing some song? *Guy* I am, OK, but *fucking asshole guy* I am not. But really I'm not thinking all this. Really when she says *I could fucking kill him* I can hear her voice a couple months back, fresh from orgasm on her dad's living room floor, and my mouth sticky and happy, her exhausted grin at me like a warm breeze, her legs bent out lazy just like I know they are sitting with her friend this second right now. *You're killing me* is what she said.

· ·

Some nights it's forgotten for a bit. A big dinner heavy in my belly maybe, reading for Modern Lit draws me in, or a test worrying me enough that I stay downstairs at the table, dad at the other end shuffling folders around from work. Quiet, my mom on the phone with her feet up, laundry piled in a basket to be folded. Or homework's done and gone, stretched out looking together at the same show, the big screen flicking at our eyes, laughing at something the famous guy says, night outside, streetlamps on the sidewalk with their *nothing to see here.* Everyone's phones silent, leaning on the pillows on the sofa like it will never hit. And then it could be the pillow, some small rub above the knee, a friction with something against something against me. Some girl in the show, some joke that zips it alive. I can blink it away for maybe thirty seconds tops, five minutes if I'm being talked at. Afraid to make a display, standing up and stretching, slow and fake when I'm already bounding upstairs in my head. And then I am bounding upstairs, my eyes full of flesh already, so it's like I don't even know if the screen's actually alive with it yet. Like a creature uncoiling from an egg, half-awake and all-hungry, the tug like an outboard motor sputtering me into the lake of sex, the family downstairs like a bear trap on my leg, as I'm excited alive and moving and very, very wanting to fuck.

Lately my favorites have the shittiest music, why is that, so I mute the stuff they give me and soundtrack it myself. It's all worked out, I move automatic to get ready. The links are hid in a place marked boring, although no one will check my computer. It only had to happen once, a quick shrieking *hey!* when I was fourteen, for my mother to now always always knock and wait for me, flinging on my loosest pants if I need to, answering and for her never to say anything like *you look a little flushed, honey* or *what's wrong you're out of breath* or *if I didn't know better I'd say you were pretty close to about to come before I knocked and spoiled it for a little just to ask if you would have some popcorn if I made some.* Nonetheless I tip my backpack sideways in front of the door so if it's opened there will be a little time-buying distraction crash. *Cole, why do you always leave your bag where anyone could trip on it, is it because you have a setup you do whenever you need to get yourself off?* Music sounds more harmless anyway, to anyone pausing outside my door, than the shuffling and nothing when I listen to the moans and dirty talk and fuck-me-harder screams through headphones on with the cord running down my bare chest against my slightly desperate beat-beating heart. Thump thump let's go on an adventure, Cole. It's nine P.M., let's watch something.

The best song for it recently is *Hello Girls,* it's by the guy, everybody knows the one, who used to be in that other thing, a party song quiet at the edges, a little lonely and of course horny, which is where I'm at. It's not a problem, which is how so many people—clergy onscreen, clingy adults—worry at it. It's not interfering or taking anything else over. It's separate from the rest of the hustle-bustle boredom that is everywhere from *wake up you'll miss the bus* to *close your eyes it's a school night.* It's like a bathroom to excuse yourself to, a corner of the house I'm stuck in, a train stop for my brain, it's just a box I need to get into by myself unless, you know, you're someone who will take my hand and lead me out of here to a better offer. Otherwise, of course, I will boot this up and watch the screens of it happening. Tap on the keys and the floodgates open bright and wet. *Hello, girls.* Hello, the clothing ripped off, the mouths kissing at it like they're trying to swallow an apple whole, the girl fierce and moaning all thirsty or, just as hot, nervous and unsure as the man, undeniable and strong, unzipping already, moves to push her down. It is not real. Nothing to do with it. What it is, what is obvious, is fucking hot. Try blonde, redhead, curly brown hair, a braid or a wig, white girls pale or freckly, every shade of black girl, hello Asian, Latina or maybe just tan, try a girl with so much makeup you can't tell what her skin is like, try someone with a big ass climbing up on the hideous sofa to ask for it. Try two girls with their toy cocks rolling over the bed. Try the man holding her ears so he can fuck her mouth, or is it too violent, just try it and see. I rub myself over my pants until they're off, inside out with the socks lagging out of the cuffs, or I will end up naked with only socks on my feet like an idiot. Try the girl on all fours, try the man turned over, try two men holding the girl's legs open so the third can be satisfied. Fake wives, fake lovers, fake babysitters, fake sluts actually fucking. Try it all, the screen offers. My cock a tent in my boxers, finally naked when one angle, one scene, one girl is the signal that it's time to go for broke. Strip off the last of it and I am as nude and excited as the day I was born. Try me, looking at my own cock trembling thick, almost a shame to touch it, an impossible move not to. This is the night in my room, and if it sounds dangerous, if you have decided it's sleazy, let me tell you it is a goddamn joy, the relentless wide-open seething tussle of all these girls helping me get off, as much as I want, as loud as I dare, free and wild and hard and happy in the juice and the dirt, until like the universe it's over with a bang and a whimper, and I close down every scene still thumping from it, the flesh looking sillier with each passing second, boxers thrown on for emergencies, rolling back my toes unclenching and the sock or the tissue or just my hand and belly sticky with the ending, eyes closed or on the ceiling with a grin or a grimace trying to gauge if I want, if I need it more, before I turn in and sleep it off, the song on its maybe third repeat. Hello, girls.

· ·

Opening my eyes when I'm kissing her, can't say why, just because it's beautiful to look at her face close up. And then she opens her eyes too. It's a thing we're doing together, her open eyes and mine, both here, both looking. Starry sky, wide over her head when she takes her shirt off. Crickets in the grass. Her dark skin, the bra a shadow over her like a cancellation. Humidity making the kisses wetter, my hands slippery flippers trying to open the stupid condom wrapper. The grass so soaked we have to pat ourselves dry a little with the sweatshirt. My eyes straining to see more, her hands straining too, on my legs. And I'm inside her. It's hot. The most fantastic thing, the two of us in the great wide-open night.

· ·

We're sending each other pictures of girls. Most of them they took themselves. Toothbrushes, hairdryers on the sink in front of the mirror as they get their lips pouty, put one leg up to show everything. Ridiculous tan lines sometimes, bright white tits like those coconut pastry balls we'd buy in sixth grade. Their boyfriends put them up to it, and then put them up here, in revenge after the breakup, for us to get hot looking at. We're playing who would you rather.

—Her.

—The blonde.

—You always like blondes.

—With an ass like that, yeah.

—Wait, there was a good ass. Here.

—Well maybe from behind so I wouldn't see her face.

—OK, her for sure, instead.

—Yeah.

—Or, wait.

And then I'm looking, fuck you Alec, at a picture of the President of the United States.

· ·

Abby was always scared of the condoms after-wards. She wouldn't touch them and she wouldn't throw them out in her house, in case her snoopy mom brush-cleared the wastebasket. So afterwards we'd walk around the neighborhood with little cloudy bundles, eggs of damp latex all tissued up, so delicate in my hand in my pocket like the baby we were trying to avoid. Nighty-night. Go to sleep in this trashcan outside the sandwich place.

. .

—You know you're a good dancer, right, Cole? You're obviously comfortable in your own body.

—Well, it's an amazing body.

Alice shoves me, and then gives me a long look.

—What?

—There's a part of your dancing I don't like.

—I can take criticism of my dancing technique.

—Stop doing it with so many other girls. I'm your girlfriend. Dance with *me*.

. .

It says next to Amateur Dorm Blow Job that thirty-five thousand people have watched it. Of course, like one thousand are me over and over.

. .

—What do you mean casual?

—I don't know. Like, not married.

—Cole, are you seeing someone else?

—No.

—Do you want to?

—I don't know.

—You don't know.

—I'm just trying to say what casual is.

—Let's talk in person.

—I can come over?

—No, call me.

—I can't come over?

—I'm not in the mood, Cole. I'm upset. Do you get that?

. .

Dammit, now against the wall her mouth is all over that guy Ada used to go with. Anna, and why not me, after the conversations I've had with you, flirty and at different times? You were not at all anytime interested, and now you picked *him*? I mean we're basically the same height, that guy and me. He even used to run on the team, we'd get each other's same sweatshirts mixed up. The only thing he has I don't have is the two of them kissing right now.

. .

Checkup time, and my doctor wants to talk about being sexual active, about sexual activity, about three more phrases they taught him to say instead of *so, are you fucking.* —Is there something you want to discuss with me?

I want to say, how about that girl in the waiting room? With the long hair?

. .

The flare-up, my fault, OK. Wondering if this will go quick or how it will go. If she can get over whatever it is to get over. And then the breakup. Her friends around her like watchdog bodyguards. Getting over *me.* Nothing on the phone. OK, OK. Official status.

So it's broken up. Dry spell, hang with Alec for a bit. The exhaustion of knowing you'll have to begin again, climb from base camp, start all over with the girl you already noticed a little bit before, saved in your pocket for later.

· ·

New semester, right away Art is a place for me. Five other boys only, two gay, one more gay but not knowing it yet, all pals-y with the girls, no competition there. Spanking new sketchbooks. Mr. Ryotis shows slides of nudes, everyone nodding all serious about the light. The light is beautiful. It's shining on an ass, also beautiful. Painters figured it out, and so smart right under everyone's noses. How many years before I can get someone to pose for me? College? I like the actual part where I draw, too.

· ·

Showered so many times at Alec's but the water pressure is weird, and the angle. It's either slapping down on your dick or your dick is totally out of the spray ignored and cold. You cannot masturbate in there, and I always wonder if this frustrates Alec, although I guess, I know, he mostly does it in his room by the computer.

And I do it sitting up on my bed now usually. Leaning on pillows. Talking to him sometimes.

. .

Nothing on Saturday night, just like Friday, so I'm back with Alec in his room calling up a movie, wondering if we both know we're going to say it's boring in an hour, and watch porn again. Or if only I just know. Our shoes are off. He burps, which is like always, but then when I catch him looking at me twenty minutes into some stupid car chase, it's something else. We turn it off.

. .

Alec sounds a little hoarse. The girls are almost slithering on the screen. We both keep shifting, our jeans crackling, weird and hot to watch it together. More weird than hot, or the other way, I don't know. He asks,
—You think there are really girls anything like that?
but the girls are right there.

. .

Alec makes a noise when he comes. I don't know what you'd call it. Not a grunt, not a moan. Nothing gross. Actually the word I guess I feel, I guess, is *cute*. I reach to hand him a tissue but he just wipes up with the T-shirt I have handy for me, I want this not to be happening and it feels so good, prickly on my skin when I think about it, and fucking hot when I don't.

. .

He's a little bigger. This is, shut up, something you have to notice.

. .

C'mon is all Alec says. C'mon. We're both in boxers. He reaches in first. His hand on my cock is the exact right weight, the rhythm perfect like never with a girl, not without showing her a few times. I say something too, but not a word I remember, or one that counts. I touch him too, it's quick and it's over like some other, any other, secret that slips into your life and then back out and you walk the world, *c'mon*, with nobody knowing.

. .

I show Kristen the painting that was projected on the wall in class. —OK. Tell me this isn't—

—Cole, you are such a perv. This is *art*. This is an *old painting*.

—He paints this party, all these naked guys chasing naked girls clutching their clothes and laughing, and *I'm* the perv?

—This was, like, *ancient* times.

—So?

—So,

but she stops. Her face is flushed a little. Her boyfriend, now finally, is walking up, that guy who has an actual beard and won third place in the whatever for I think chemistry. She doesn't care now, not as much, about arguing with me, and suddenly the sex conversations are private. He makes her come, probably I'm sure, too early to give up her virginity but they get naked and afterwards I bet she giggles and clutches her clothes. *Ancient times.* Ancient times to her is when she was single and thought I was a sex monster.

—I guess you're leaving now.

—Yeah, see ya, Cole.

I'm alone on the bench with this painting in this book. The lawn so green. And if we had a party like that they would send us all to jail.

· ·

We're sitting closer, hands in each other's boxers again. Don't know why we keep them on, or what that's about. Don't know what any of it's about. I won't kiss him but I think he's tried a couple of times. Leaned in so I could see a couple places he missed shaving. His face so very close up. Yes, I really don't know what it is that is happening.

· ·

—We could try.

He says this just when I knew he would. Onscreen a girl is watching two guys touching. "Wife Turns Husband Bi."

It's more than a month since any girl has been around to do anything with. I'm just thinking. Prison, guys do it in prison in the same situation.

· ·

Alec has a nice body, I guess, I don't even know what I'm saying or what I mean by that. Compared to that other guy, I guess, over there. Either of them. Boys, hello.

. .

—You don't have to.

His mouth was already on me, my hand trying to grab something of his. It seemed only fair.

—I'll just do you.

OK, but wondering if I owed him.

. .

When we were done, gradually it felt too cold, but pulling up a blanket over us felt too married and sweetheart and gay. Alec sat up suddenly and said the name of a two-player game, soldier partners blowing up zombies.

—Yeah. Let's.

Kicked our pants on. Relieved it could be normal.

. .

Look at it this way, I am theorizing to myself taking a run. It's an experiment. Experimenting. And then like a science fair, the experiment will be over. Sweaty when the second mile's over, knowing I could do the maybe half-mile to his house and that he, like not any other no way ever girl, would take me up to his room quick and hot without a shower. But that's like a boyfriend move, I think. That's not an experiment bored one single night, that's something else. And I am running, I find myself realizing, down the last block, to his house.

. .

The first Monday after the first time, I watch Alec watching what's-her-name bend over to get something out of her bag on the floor. It's a deep wide relief. Still into girls, me too, everything's cool.

. .

I move my hand up his leg and he makes a noise, then frowns and opens his eyes.

—What was that?

—What?

He's looking at me. —That noise you made.

—You're crazy.

—You made a noise—

—That was *you*, Alec.

But in a second I'm making it again.

. .

I had five orgasms in a day and it was easy and not the first or last time. First straight out of a morning dream about a girl with whispering lips on all fours. Second in the shower, remembering to put the conditioner in first so it's working on my hair while I do it. After school with Alec twice, I guess the phrase would be *via mouth*. Once more lounging around after homework with two girls on the screen helping out. And then I'm spacing out halfway hearing some interview guy saying he goes *crazy* if it doesn't happen once a week and, *once a week?* I would have gone six, seven if they'd allowed it in Applied Econ.

· ·

One time, maybe it's the beer he had, Alec and I are laughing so hard we have to stop. Heaving with it. Feeling better than coming, well almost, to get it out like this. Alec is sputtering on the floor trying to choke it out, slapping me lightly and laughing, laughing.

C-C-C-C- he tries. *Cocksucker.*

· ·

—Hang tonight?

I tell him yeah. —What are we going to do?

Three benches over, Alec just glances at me quick, and it's enough to know. I knew anyway. He puts his phone in his pocket. What I mean is, I want it, and I want him not to say anything about it, and I'm getting them both.

. .

He swallows it all and then, his eyes wide and laughy, slides off me leaving me pulsing and gleaming and laughing at him on his bedroom rug with his arms joking raised up like an athlete. Like a champ.

. .

—We could try.

It's late. Computer's gone to some geometric design Alec set up, waving slow across the screen in the blue light. I'm trembling, wired and tired. He has half a bed sheet over him but I have refused it, just naked with boxers very handy if someone, they never would, walks in. He puts it a different way before I can say no.

—I would let you try.

· ·

—Condom.

It's dark when he says this. The word sounds serious. It's a real word, it makes the whole thing real even in the dark.

—What?

—Dude, don't *what*. I know where you've been, Cole.

His voice has a muffle to it so for just one spooky second I think he's crying. But his face, I realize then, is just buried in the pillow as he waits for me to put it on. He says it again.

—Condom.

—Ssh, yes.

· ·

He feels good. It feels good with him but also, half-curled up against him when it's over, kids in the neighborhood shrieking around on bikes ringing little bells on the street out his window, he feels good. And, he says he feels good and I don't like that. I don't want to tell him, out of all the people I shouldn't have to tell, that he should count on me like the rusty car across the street half-covered by a tarp in the neighbor's driveway, for zero, for nothing, nothing at all. I don't say this, can't, me freaking out slowly next to him and my hands, his hands, moving and wanting it again.

. .

We do it again. We keep doing it.

. .

So it's like with a girl, I guess. I'm running again, thinking it through. And like with a girl you don't say, I don't think I like you anywhere in the neighborhood of where you like me, but the sex is delicious and you're also, yes you're cool. But he's a guy. And dude, *Cole*, a friend.

. .

—We could try.

It's the thing Alec keeps on saying. We *are,* I want to say back. I *am.* Trying, I'm trying it. But he means something else. I'm trying it like, you find a coin on the table and you spin it for no reason but to see it happen.

He's trying it like medical school, because maybe he'll
grow up to be a doctor.

. .

—That,
Alec says it breathless.
—was the *best.*
My head is like a spider on a beach ball, trying to
wrap around it that I basically used the same trick Ava
taught me, the one I always used on girls. He is trembling.
—The best.

. .

Then Kristen almost sniffs it out of me one sudden
day.
—You haven't had a girlfriend in how long? And
you're calm and not sleazy.
—Thanks.
—No, I mean it's weird. You haven't even dirty-
joked at me.
—If I was seen joking with you your boyfriend
would beard me to death.

—Jealous.

—Ha!

—I know, you have a secret lover.

—Shut up.

—What's her name?

—Shut up.

—*His* name? Ha ha.

—Shut up. My secret lover is you, but you sleep right through it. You know how you wake up on your stomach?

—OK, you're back to normal, dickhead.

. .

We go out sometimes, too. Not *go out*. But not in his room, driving somewhere and suddenly he smells different. Alec put on cologne—this can *not*, better not be for me.

. .

I could ask the drama teacher I guess, or they say Mr. Marzada although it doesn't seem like it. A gay teen help phone line *twenty-four hours ask any question, someone is listening, someone is here for you,* tacked up outside the nurse's office. Though I don't know what it is, I mean, that I'd be asking.

• •

Walking back to his place, our hands keep brushing and we both keep jumping back from it. I mean even if we wanted to, it is not quite the world here of 100 percent nobody will beat the shit out of you, two guys holding hands.

Or, at least, *I* am jumping away.

• •

—We could,

I know he's going to say it.

—go out.

—We do go out, Alec.

—Yeah.

—We were at Drew's party yesterday night.

—Yeah.

—I'm not gay, by the way.

—Fuck you, I'm not either.

—OK.

—But maybe bi.

—I'm not.

—OK but Cole.

—Fuck you.

—Yeah exactly, like what we have? Look it up. Sex is the word for it.

—Yeah I know.

—So I'm saying bi, OK? I said it for me.

But the word, I want to say, for me is mostly *horny.*

· ·

And then I met Grisaille.

· ·

Out in front of school, she shrugged up her arms, and I saw all the hair she had in her armpits. She tugged her sweater on while I looked at her lips, and I started wondering who I could ask to find out who she was because I knew there was no way she'd been here all along. But Grisaille just turned her head and imitated me, a big dumb staring monkey look, and then smiled and beckoned me over.

· ·

—Anna says you're Cole.

—Yeah. Hi.

—Hi. Now you ask my name.

—OK.

—OK, what?

—OK, what's your name?

And then before she told me she gave me a champion smile, like it was too easy, making me ask in my shuffling shoes.

· ·

She looked so fucking fantastic agreeing to go out with me. She didn't look like a girl who would ruin the whole thing *at all*. Beautiful, breasty, like so warm to roll around in was my first impression. And, the next seventy thousand impressions.

We don't have girls like this, is what I wanted to say to her. And thank God I didn't.

· ·

—Yeah, there's stuff to do in this town. My friend, next weekend, is having a thing.

—I'm only here for the semester, Cole, so we're going to have to make this quick. Friday night?

—Tomorrow?

—Open the thing. There. I'm putting my number in your phone. Figure it out.

It was in a shirt pocket. She had to scratch my chest a little through the flannel to get my phone out. I felt her nail there still, like an itch. But my mouth was just saying stupid *Tomorrow?* again.

· ·

Her skirt ended short and she had black, not stockings, ripped socks. Skin, is what she had. She kept rubbing her own legs while we sat there on that bench talking, with me thinking, who dropped you here into my lap like this?

· ·

Alec and I are looking her up and talking about it.

—Scroll down. Look, she's on a beach with a bunch of guys who look older.

I squint, blink at the hairy chests. —They don't look older, they're just Arabic.

—That's funny, because the photo says it was a beach party in Costa de Lisboa which . . . screen says . . . is in Portugal.

—Yeah, her dad is Portuguese. But he's in Berlin now.

—And how do you pronounce again—

—Grizz-eye. But some people pronounce it like it rhymes with *awhile*.

—Is that what she told you?

—Yeah.

—Did it sound that amazing when she said it? It sounds like it would sound amazing. *Rhymes with awhile.*

—I saw her first.

—She saw *you*, is what you told me. It's like a movie, some foreign girl comes to town. I honestly don't even think it occurred to me that girls could have hair there in their armpits. I mean, *possible*, but not happening. Even in the *bushiest* porn—

—Alec, shut up and where were we?

—Grizz-eye. Portugal.

—OK, Portugal.

—Why has she lived all these places? And why now our lame place?

—Divorce. Her mom's from here, or used to be.

—And married, wow, look who she married. Follow the link. Her dad looks like the guy in those brandy commercials.

—Rum.

—OK, but he's handsome.

—I will pretend you didn't say that. He's a dick anyway, she says. All he cares about is expensive paintings and stuff.

—Art dealer. *Aggressive Art Dealer Taking Barcelona by Storm.* You think he's really smuggling heroin?

—No, because we're not all in a low-budget thriller.

—OK, he's actually handsome, you gotta admit.

I'm stuck on the beach party Alec found. There are a lot of guys in it, around her.

—You're admitting it.

—Shut up Alec. Don't be gay.

—Fuck you.

—Sorry.

—Seriously.

—Sorry.

—OK. Do you want to come over?

. .

Grisaille brings it up right right right away.

—You know you have a rep, right?

—Rep?

—It's short for reputation, Cole.

—I know what it means but what do you mean?

—They say, you fuck anything that moves.

I flushed a little looking at the phone. Out the window it was windy. Everything was moving. If only.

—It's not true.

—I think it is. A girl at lunch was counting on her fingers and she ran out of fingers.

—Well, how many fingers does she have?

Grisaille's laugh is like when you're a kid, and adults are having a party you hear downstairs, stylish and wine. Her voice is not done laughing when she tells me,

—I had a rep too, sometimes.

—Sometimes?

—Of course, they didn't call it *a rep*.

—What did they call it?

She pauses and I'm listening to her breathe. In the static I grasp that what I'm wondering is what *she* will call it, having a rep. Maybe I've already blown it with her, like cops call it onscreen: *prior bad acts*. Her voice is quiet, or maybe it's just the way I'm listening to it.

—*We* could call it anything.

· ·

You'll do, is what she said when we were done kissing that time. You'll do fine.

· ·

—Cole, do you have a favorite German poet?

—

—I said, do you—

—Sorry, I thought you were kidding. Let me answer for everyone you will ever meet in this town, no, we don't have favorite German poets. We have favorite diners and beers.

—School last year, we all had to pick one. I got Rilke and I'm finishing my translation unit.

—But you go here now.

—I just want to do it. He wrote these elegies that are all about love and sex.

—Are you, sometimes you don't even seem like a real person compared to everyone.

Grisaille's mouth, unspeakably sexy, as she laughs.

—What do you mean, Cole?

Sexy, is the word I think, but it's too gawky a word, not old-fashioned enough. The word I find is

—*Glamorous.*

—That's a good word, Cole. Maybe you can help me with the last translation.

But *sexy* was the right word all along.

· ·

Awake in the morning zippy and hard, like my cock can't wait to see her the most.

Exactly like that, come to think of it.

· ·

—That was a good kiss. Give me more of that.

She was the first girl to ask for more so greedily. Or ever. I opened my mouth wider.

—More.

This was the first date.

—Can you take me somewhere?

· ·

—You have a reputation.

—Yeah, you keep saying.

—You have not been a gentleman with many girls.

The word *gentleman* stands in the air like a time traveler. —We don't call it that, *gentleman.*

—Yes but I think you know what I mean. And it's true?

—I guess it's true. I don't think of it like that.

—So how do you think of it, Cole?

—Um, that I'm practicing?

—For what?

—For you.

She could not help laughing very loud. But an hour later she had her bra off. Someday you'll learn your lesson, maybe eight girls have said to me. But most of them got naked.

. .

A single mother like Grisaille's, the greatest blessing you can give a boyfriend. Works all day, extra hours for the piles of bills on the counter, and out a lot at night. Drinks sometimes, when she gets home from a date tipsy, doesn't notice what liquor's missing or swigged from.

Of course, on the other hand, a mom like this basically hates men, and sees right through you, and lives in hysteria of the girl getting pregnant. So it goes both ways.

. .

—It clasps in front.

—In—? Oh.

—It was funny what you were doing back there, though. I know what it's like to be a back door in a bad neighborhood, the way you scuffled at it. You could just say, take off your bra.

—Take off everything.

—Whoa cowboy. You're not a hypnotist.

. .

She's right there suddenly. Alec and I have met up at the failing coffee place by the almost-done condos. He is holding two bags of pretzels, he wants to go to his house and talk about the details. Grisaille. I say her name, first to him and then to her. She strolls over and puts her hand on my arm. —I had fun last night.

—Yeah.

—Did you get my—

—I haven't had my phone all day.

I say this with my phone in my pocket, but Grisaille only smiles.

—Are you doing something later?

—Later? This is Alec, by the way.

—Hi.

—Hi, Grisaille.

—Later?

—Later? No.

—Good, call me.

She's at the door with two big iced teas, must be her mom in the car. I turn back and Alec is looking at me with the pretzels still, drooping now though. He knows it already.

．．

Second real date, she asked if it was cold out. She ran back up to her room with me to get a sweater, but as soon as we got there she unbuckled me and put me in her mouth. The feeling of it, hardening against her tongue, twice as big as she slipped me out of her lips to look at me, holy fuck. Then she sucked me in earnest and I came quick. Ssh, she said, although we were alone in the house. Then she zipped me up and we went out the door kissing with my taste in her mouth.

—I really liked that.

She was talking in my ear.

—Yes.

—Yes?

She was laughing but I still couldn't. —Me too I mean.

—Let's not stay too late k? I'll want my turn.

—K,

I was stuttering it out. —K, —K, —K, —K,

• •

—You know her name's not a real name, right Cole? You know it's some art technique or whatever?

—Her dad named her. A really famous painter suggested it, and—

—OK, but it's *not. A real. Name.*

It unnerves Alec, for some reason, to hang out with her practically at all. He was fine with the other girls, sexy even to know he knew the details while we just hung out talking, but for some reason not now, for some reason this is for some reason different. I mean, I know what the reason is, I guess. I know I know it.

• •

Her mom picks her up at my house. She runs right out. I wave at both of them zipping away, my breath clouding it up when I rest my face on the cold pane. Her taste in my breath, then on the window alone.

. .

Supposed to be reviewing the rules of the argumentative essay, day after the second date. Her mouth on my cock, so deep, right when I walked in the door. My homework rustles. Pros and cons. Cons, I guess, is that if she were really sucking me *all the time* it would be hard to do anything else. But holy fuck the pros.

. .

I call her and she says she just came.
—What? Like touching yourself?
She finishes the sip of water. —Home. Shopping with my mom. What did you say?
—Hi. I said hi.
—Hi, Cole.

. .

—You know her name's not a real name?
—You told me this a thousand times.

—What kind of name is that even anyway?

I sigh at Alec and type back. —Different from all the other girls.

—It's really different, freaky.

Alec, you have no idea.

. .

—Do guys like it when the girl talks dirty?

Her teeth are a little purple from red wine. Never knew there was such a thing ever, a girl who drinks red wine.

—Guys?

I'm trying not to think of Alec. There was some dirty talk, sure.

—You, then. Do you like it? You want me to talk like a whore?

She leans in and whispers in my ear. —150 for oral, 300 for a straight fuck.

—Beat it, I'm a cop.

Big purple laugh.

. .

Out up on the hill, haven't been here in forever, wind and leaves moving across the junky scraggle of a field. A lost squirrel goes by quick.

—I keep living so many places, Cole. Everyone I ever met at every school just starts to blur by. I follow them and see their parties on the screen, and it's just like some old scenery I passed. You know? You don't. You live here. But another semester, a year. I just keep moving and there's no real place, no destination.

I'm loving her suddenly. I feel it in my throat and my pulse keeps thumping.

—I could be it.

She kisses me and I taste the chocolate she likes, found a forgotten square in the coat she bought on a weekend in London.

—You could be.

She moves my hand to her breast.

· ·

Third date her mom was out again, and we just had some toast downstairs, hardly talking. Up to her room, she took off all her clothes before we even started. I thought I would look away, but I didn't,

—Cole, get naked, I want you naked.
and then I did.

. .

—It's one thing to write love poems.

She's holding a sheet of paper over us, like a strict, square cloud. We're on our backs in bed looking at it.

—That's the poem? The real first line?

—Yeah.

—*It's one thing to write love poems?* That's cool, actually.

—I told you, Cole. It's one thing to write love poems. Another, however, to deal with that deity of the river of blood.

—See, *that* sounds more like poetry that I was thinking.

—You mean it's bad.

—Oh, I forgot you—

—Yeah, I translated. But it *is* bad, it sounds ridiculous. There's another part where the real translation is *godhead*, I have to make that also not ridiculous.

—Well, go on.

—Really?

—Yeah, really. What did you think?

The paper sinks down. She curls my leg over hers.

—Even the girl, who thinks she knows her young lover . . .

—Why did you ask me over that time?

—The first time? I don't know, we just met, right? Maddy introduced us?

—No, you just beckoned me over.

—Before that, we met at lunch. No, wait, maybe I was just looking at you. I remember your jeans were too tight.

—What?

—Your black ones, Cole. How could you not know that, the way that was. Even she isn't close enough for him to tell how this lord of lust.

—You're kidding about that. Lord of lust?

Her leg keeps rubbing over me. I'm getting thicker and thicker. The line about my jeans too tight, it's working.

. .

Done with homework, or half-done anyway. Think of a good search term, *amateur outdoors*. Hello, girls. Then her name comes up on the screen. Still not used to seeing it.

—What are you up to?

I shut all the naked windows. —Nothing you?

—To be honest I was masturbating.

Hard to type "whoawhoawhoaohmygodwhat" so I type nothing.

—Not super successfully, though. Can you call me? Are you alone?

My pants are already uncomfortable as I walk to lay my backpack across the door.

—Yeah one sec.

—Are you hard, Cole?

Fingers on the phone, I'm saying it out loud to the waiting screen. —One sec one sec one sec . . .

· ·

She speaks up for it, the sex. It's not just something she *lets me do* or *enjoys*. It's something she wants and asks for. Actually, she's like that, I am seeing, about everything, and it's exciting. It's spooky.

· ·

She shows up one morning bounding into school with a quick kiss and a motorcycle helmet, shiny black like a smooth globe of a blank new planet, tucked under her arm trying to look like no big deal. She cannot help grinning no matter how long she's lived in Europe.

—My mom let me have it for the day. I'm taking you on a ride after school.

We'd already had sex, but that afternoon with the howling wind, my fingers clenched on her back real hard, the shriek in my ears rushing by and the cooped-up sight with my eyes locked on her back, reined-in with terror and the buzz, the stupendous vibing of the thrum of the shiver of the engine all up between my legs pushing its electrics through my throttling spine to my gasping teeth, the dismount onto the gravel of the rest stop to be tugged through damp trees to the woods shady and chilly on the damp ground, ripping the wrapper open while she smiles with her jeans off and socks on, that was the first time we *fucked.*

. .

—Officially together?

She repeats this in the tone of what's-the-problem-officer. I already thought it might not work, to ask her.

—OK.

—Do we need a permit, Cole? Do I have to pay for the whole year up front?

—I was just asking.

—Can we just, play it as it goes along, by ear?

And, like a sock to the stomach, I get how every previous girl felt looking and asking that question, officially, at me.

. .

We walk in together to a party, and it's like they can smell it on us. She must have told some girl who told everyone. I get high-fivey nods from guys I don't know. Girls only talk to me about her. We dance a little but everyone is wondering why don't we just leave. We have a car. Lords of lust. We should be in it fucking.

. .

—You're with Grisaille now? Officially.

Alec was waiting where we meet up sometimes, mad. He hadn't answered the last couple times but I hadn't thought about it. —Yeah.

—And you didn't tell me. It's officially, and you didn't—

—I did tell you. What, Alec, the fuck? Is it the details you want?

He shoved me, a real shove, and then scraped at his eyes a little. —Fuck you.

—What?

—Figure it out.

He was already stalking away toward the gate. What are the rules on this? If he was a girlfriend, I would try more onscreen, *I'm a dick* or *sorry* or *Are you OK are we OK now?* or try to hack it out through his friends. But his friends are me, and guys I wouldn't ever talk to about *anything*, and besides he is not, not, not my fucking girlfriend.

. .

—S, A . . .

I tell her she's wrong already. —It wasn't even S.

—Felt like S. Do it again.

—I love your eyes when I do this.

—It feels like finger painting.

—It's not finger painting. I'm writing a real word on your back. Guess.

—L.

—Not L.

—Don't make me guess, Cole. It could be anything. Just keep writing.

And I do. I keep writing, and not just, I'm thinking, the dirty parts. There's more.

. .

—So you lived in Cairo and Lisbon.

—Italy as a kid. Germany for, I guess it was, one semester, and then back again.

—Like here.

—Well, not much like here.

I lean into her belly, the smell so warm and strange with something girls at my high school do not wear, do not smell like. Familiar, foreign at the same time, like someone I literally dreamed up. —Did you have a guy in Germany?

—Cole.

—I'm just asking.

—You want me to start that, *you? You* who can't be in the same room or else Adrienne will tear you limb from limb she hates you so much?

. .

—What are you doing?

I stop it, I was nervous about it anyway. —Sorry.

—No, no, go ahead. I'm just curious.

. .

—You're a beautiful girl.

—I don't know.

—What? You are.

—*Girl* feels weird.

—You're a beautiful *woman*.

—No, no, now I'm old when you say that like that.

—Well not *girl* not *woman*, I don't know—
She moves close. —Just say beautiful.
And I do.

. .

—Keep your panties on.

—What?

—Keep—

—But how could we—

—I'll pull them aside, leave them on.

—OK . . .
She stands up with a ridiculous, ridiculously *sexy*
smile. — . . . If *you* wear one shoe, and both of these
barrettes . . .

. .

Kristen waves her hand in front of my face. —Group project. Not, Kristen does it while you think about your girlfriend.

—OK, shut up, OK.

—She is something to think about, though. You've met your match with that one.

I say it dirtily so she'll shut up maybe. —A perfect fit.

She just rolls her eyes. Nothing's dirty to her now, not in month four, is it, with Mark and his beard. —She could snap you in two, Cole. She probably has, come to think of it.

. .

We sit at the donut place all day after school. I have an English paper I totally spaced and Grisaille is at her phone and drawing birds on napkins. Her bare wrist brushes me and I remember her skin and look up slow, her leg tendrilled up with mine now, the epic happy, so calm, that there's so much time with her stretched out, plenty to finish this moment before we go home to her room.

. .

Rob runs into me in the parking lot.

—You're with that Spanish girl now?

—She's not Spanish. She just lived in Lisbon for a while with her dad, so actually—

—Yeah. But you're with her? How is that?

We've hung out a thousand times but always in a pack. I know maybe two things about Rob—he plays football, and last year punched some guy's arm, I don't remember the rest. I try to make up a way to talk to him. —The best fuck.

He grimaces and keeps walking. —Dude. I just meant, is she nice.

. .

—It's one thing to write love poems. Another, though, to deal with that river-god of the blood: hidden, guilty. Even the girl, who thinks she knows her young lover, even she isn't close enough for him to tell how this lord of lust, in the lonely times before she knew him, before she eased him, almost before she seemed possible, would lift up his godhead . . .

I wasn't laughing but now I am, just a little. —Sorry.

She smiles but she is almost, actually, sad about it. —I know. Still ridiculous.

—It wasn't, until that word.

—Yeah, but do you know what it is? Godhead?

I squint my eyes to last year's Lit class. I was hardly there then, what with Amelie when her mom went away for ten days. —Godhead. Isn't it—

but then I'm shrieking. She's grabbing my cock, almost joysticky, and waving it around.

—wet with the utterly unknown, and churn the night—

—Ouch ouch ouch!

—to an endless riot! Ha!

. .

Alec's wide lonely eyes actually turn my stomach one day in the hall. —We haven't hung out in a while.

—We hang out all day every day all school day long.

—Maybe this weekend you want to,

—She and I will probably go to Luka's party.

—She and I.

—Alec, she's my girlfriend.

But he's just looking at me. —Alec.

—I guess I thought . . .

But he doesn't finish it. I have to tell him, so what I say is, —But I told you, we weren't.

. .

I looked on the computer and there's a scale for it, gay to straight and you can be anywhere on it. I'm on it at the part of, if there's no girl why not, and now there is, so let's stop and be cool about it.

He's at, obviously, some other part.

. .

And the person I would talk about it to, this Alec situation or mess or nothing, would be Alec. My hand hovers on the screen. Grisaille doesn't answer, so now I don't have to decide whether or not to talk about it with Grisaille, I scroll through my others, almost laughable how I will never tell any of them any of this.

. .

Even the girl who thinks she knows her young lover, even she isn't close enough for him to tell—

. .

Let's watch something. Hello, look at this girl bent over the table. Four years ago I think, I thought anal sex just meant you were really particular about it.

.   .

She calls in the morning. —Run over here.

—I have the car though.

—But I want you sweaty, Cole. Record-break the two-mile, that run.

.   .

—Get on top of me.

—No, no, Cole. Keep like this. Keep moving. Yes.

—But I want—

—Don't care what you want, keep moving, yes, yes, yes, yes, fuck, yes, yes.

.   .

—I want to watch us in the mirror, Cole, but I need my glasses.

The Venn diagram of adorable and fuckable, in the mirror with glasses on and nothing else, her legs up against my chest, grinning until I push deeper and she has to close her eyes.

. .

—Stop covering it up. It's cutest now.

—Now?

—It's cute. Like a little slug when it's done. Don't get me wrong, it's hot when it's big. But your little resting cock, so cute. Adorable godhead.

—Still ridiculous, that word.

—Well, you can't put *penis* in a poem, right? Also ridiculous. *Cock?* Oh, you're ruining it.

—*You're* ruining it. It's your talk that did it.

—So much for cute.

—But it's hot now?

—Yes. Getting there.

. .

I press in deeper. It's further but it's not closer. Not the latex, just the separateness, some other distance I can't slide across. Grisaille feels the same, I can tell, her legs urging me on. But we can't, we need to, get closer than this, can we? Can we? Is there a trick to it, a technique that will make this as wild and together as I know we are feeling? Is there? I am almost crying at how far away from it we are finding ourselves, on this trembling actual bed.

. .

She got up and went to the bathroom and came back wearing only my shirt. I was on my back on the bed. She stopped at the edge of the bed and clutched my hair a little. Then she moved so she was on my mouth and just rubbed there. Her moans were so unpretty I knew it was real. She tasted like everything, like a girl, like a person, like a creature. Midway I tried to reach for her and she said no and like this came on my mouth like I wasn't even there and I, so much, loved it.

. .

I would like to excuse my son Cole from school this morning. I could see at breakfast that he had spent Sunday afternoon fucking and fucking and needs to spend today thinking about it and masturbating and recuperating.

. .

We kiss hard in the vitamin aisle and then there's an old man scowling at us. Leave us alone. This is, have you *seen* her body, what we're for, to be messing around if we want to.

. .

And every time she walks up to me it's another motorcycle ride.

. .

—Wait, you're,

—What?

—Your arm, if you could,

—You're acting like I'm in the *way*, Cole. Like I'm smack dab in the middle of your path—

—Well,

—of fucking me, Cole. *Me. Hello.*

—OK. Put your arm anyplace you want then.

And I'm shrieking out of the bed while she howls with giggles.

—Not there!

—You said *anyplace*!

. .

I flunked a test, a big one. Rain makes me cranky anyway, angry even. Alec acted like a dick all day. I know my mom's going to give me shit. I am telling Grisaille these things lying on her floor, for her to get down from the bed and make me feel better. Days like today, I am telling her how much I really need to come.

. .

When I come on her belly she lounges and dips one finger in, moves around like a skater. We name the babies that have not happened. Mildred. Helga. Skippy. Nobody we'll ever know.

. .

—Would you pose for me?
—Like naked? No way, Cole.
—But I'm looking at you naked now.
—One, I have a sock on. And for two, you couldn't draw me. You'd just pounce on me in five minutes.
—No I wouldn't.

—Yes you would, look. You're hard talking about it. The word *pounce*, that was hot.

. .

I am playing with her hair. Of all the girls, hers is my world's favorite to play with.

—Out of all the girls—

—Ssh, ssh, don't say anything, don't spoil it.

—I was just always looking for you.

She sighs a little. She puts a shirt on. She's right, I wrecked it.

. .

—We can't do it standing up if we're not the same height, Cole. Not really.

I stop and need to process how offhand she is, knowing this. Some experience in Germany, up against a wall with some other boy. Kind of hot, kind of sickening. She looks at me and misreads it.

—Cole, you know I'm taller, right? A little taller. Other fucks. Better fucks than me.

. .

—So you pose for *me*, Cole.

I'm already up. —OK.

—Let me get my sketchbook. This pen sucks. OK, put your arm up.

—What? Why?

—Because it changes your belly, see?

—Don't draw my belly.

—I'm drawing . . .

The pen busy, her eyes hungry with it —*everything*, Cole.

· ·

Birds fighting on a tree out my window. Really fighting, not cute, flutter and feather and weird soft hoarse noises. She's not worth it, I want to tell them, but she probably is.

· ·

—If we start down low on the bed, your head won't end up against the wood.

—I don't care.

—Doesn't it—

—I don't care, Cole, if it hurts sometimes.

. .

Because I don't feel safe with her I guess. It feels, not dangerous, but with no seatbelt, no helmet, hanging onto her on that roaring motorcycle day after night after day. I feel endangered a little, probably looking at her the way, Alana was it, Abby, used to look at me when I realized her brother wasn't around and we could go up to her room. *Safe*, everyone says about sex. Everyone says everyone should feel *safe*. I always did, but they never, not quite, I think, I know. My turn, with Grisaille. I can't always say I like it. But it's very, don't-touch-that, *hot*.

. .

—Make me spaghetti.

It's a rainy afternoon. We are under a blanket with both our pants pushed down but not off. Everywhere is sticky with it.

—Is that a euphemism?

I am hoping. She pokes me. —Spaghetti.

—I can't cook at all, ever.

She elbows herself up to look at me like a cheap broken something, not worth the money to fix. —Look

it up on a phone. Boil water. Put it on a plate. Make
me spaghetti and Cole, I will show you a new trick
I do—
    But I'm already in the kitchen, pulling my pants up.

· ·

    —I really,
    She's rolling off me with an enormous smile.
    —I really enjoy fucking.
    I feel the flushiness on my face. I stumble out the
word, —Good.
    —I mean, I really enjoy it as an activity.
    —Well, that's good.
    —It is *very* good. Don't you like it?
    I raise my hands. —Eh. It's OK.
    She crawls back and nips me on the face. —Then I!
Must! Fuck! You! Better!

· ·

    —There's gum in my bag I think.
    A girl's bag is an abandoned warehouse. Stupid people
in horror movies are the only ones to venture in. I
plunge anyway, a tattered pursey thing with old thick

buckles and the lining frayed like a mongoose tried to get out. Rise above the tampons. Wallet, pen, here's the gum and then the thing small and plastic in my hand like a ring of shivery light.

—I was going to tell you.

—You're on the pill?

—Just started.

—How did you, um?

—How did I what? They're pills. You put them in your mouth. Every day, there's a schedule. See, little days of the week on the thing. If you're not diseased—

—I'm not. My doctor checks, without telling my mom, which is cool.

—The clinic's like that.

—The clinic.

—It's on, what's the street, near the overpass.

—There's protestors sometimes. Guys yelling.

She shrugs a little, her mouth wrestly on her gum.

—There's another entrance. If you call ahead.

I didn't know, slightly, at all, what I was saying.

—Isn't it, but why—

—It's OK there. I mean, not my idea of a good time, an exam.

—So why,

It was a smile, I guess, but mostly it was—determined, is

what she is like, looking at me. —Because, Cole, it's worth it.

. .

It's one thing to write love poems.

. .

She moans face down like a devout prayer, naked with her bra on. My tongue moves all over her legs and her hand cheats up to masturbate. I mean, this is something I never even thought to search for online.

. .

—Show me the porn you look at.
—No absolutely no never no.
—C'mon. Here? Tell me what site.
—I am not doing this.
—A lot of pigtails here. You like this?
—No.
But she was already pigtailing herself. It was our first fight, my first fight ever that left me still mad after the sex.
—I was just curious. I just wanted to know how it is for you. It's OK you masturbate.

—I. Do. Not. Want. To.

—Talk to me, Cole.

—Talk. About it.

. .

She can draw, and she can dress well, and she can make me come so hard with her mouth, but holy fuck she cannot sing. It is like a joke about a puppet show when the song comes on she likes. I turn it up. The song's OK but so loud it drowns her out.

. .

Saving me money and shame she says —Can you believe some girls, at this school, get from their boy-friends, *stuffed animals?*

—I know, right?

I am trying not to be astonished when I say this. So many girls, so many, cooing at the little kitten or what-ever. The money for bunnies I have spent, and Grisaille, so beautiful rolling her eyes. This isn't that.

—It's pervy how little kid it is. Look Anna, Daddy got you a teddy bear.

. .

—I have my period.

I force nothing onto my face for her. I know enough what *not* to say, but the right thing I haven't learned.

—OK, we can just—

—No, I want to do it, Cole. But we need two things. We need a towel, and for you not to freak out.

. .

—Who? Maddy?

—No . . .

—Tell me. I'm new here. There is so much, you would not believe, gossip about you. So, Kaitlin?

—Yes.

She squealed.

—We didn't go all the way.

—Alice?

—Alice White or Alice Davenport?

—Both.

—Yes. Stop squealing.

—Anne-Marie.

—Yes.

—Amber.

—No. Well, once.

—Why don't you list them all?

—Why don't *you?*

—OK.

She curled up against me. We both had our socks on, the weird texture of it, cotton and jealousy.

—OK, first was Marco. He was very hairy.

—Please let's do something else.

. .

She's at the bus stop typing to me. —Nothing personal Cole but guys are assholes. Three dudes here with hip-hop so loud, shouting over and over, suck my nuts, suck my nuts.

—Well, are you going to do it?

She snaps a picture of her middle finger which even like that looks gorgeous to me.

. .

Kristen wants to ask me something.

—OK.

She sighs, rattles her fingers on the desk. Mark went and got her a ring, clacky and blue. Not what I like, but if you like that sort of thing. —Forget it.

—What?

—Forget it.

—OK, I forgot it. But what did you want to ask me?

She pokes me, then sighs. Takes off the ring for a second. If I was Mark seeing this, I would *uh-oh*. —You're a guy.

—That's what's on your mind? Yeah, I am. Thought you'd never ask, Kristen.

—Shut up. But do you, I can't believe I'm asking.

—What what?

She looks away from me and then looks at me and away and a few more times before she exhales, and, —Do you love them?

—What?

—*Did*, I mean. Did you love them. All the girls, and now Grisaille. When you say *I love you*, and I know you do sometimes, is it real, did you mean it—

—Kristen—

—or is it just a thing to say?

I start to answer, but it's an answer for the team. Then I see her look. In her eyes is a kid too old for a magician,

not knowing how it's done but wise to the trick that the coin is not, of course, plucked supernaturally from her ear. So the truth, is what I decide, OK yes, to spill.
—Both.

—Both? It can't be both, Cole. Either you love a girl, a *person*, or you don't, and you're just trying to stay, I don't know. *Coupled. Laid.*

—You're going to call me perv if I answer this, Kristen laughs. —Probably.

—or worse. But *coupled* and *laid*, this is love, right?

—It's just a part of it.

—OK, but a big part.

—For guys maybe.

—Yeah, but Kristen, that's like half the world.

—What about my half?

—You don't like *coupled* and *laid?* I've known you for what, we met the first day of school. You are happiest *now.* With that guy. *Coupled* and *laid.* It's a very big happiness. So, yes, we say things. To keep happiness going.

She's chewing on her sleeve. —You don't mean them.

—Of course we absolutely mean it. You don't *accidentally* buy a girl a ring. You mean to do it. You go to the store, you open your stupid wallet. Believe me, he means it, your boyfriend. He wants you both to be happy. *And, yes,* sorry but not really, not really sorry, *laid.*

She's looking at me, this girl, and boy do I know this look. There are nicer ways to put it, what this look is, the way buying a shiny ring could be called *generosity* instead of *keeping Mark laid.* The look is disillusioned, maybe. Disappointed. Kind of very sad but just a little. But the way I think of this look, and it's dirty, is that she's sorry she ever opened her legs.

. .

—But you're leaving at the end of the year, right?

—*Cole.* This is February.

—But you're leaving then. Going back.

—Cole, you're pouting.

—I'm not . . .

—How many girls are you with in what, five months?

—This is different.

—Maybe, maybe it is. Five weeks.

—I'm just asking.

—Don't miss me already when I'm right here. Next year when you're lonely you can find me and we'll wave to our little cameras.

Another girl on a screen. I'm glad she can't see me freak out a little.

. .

Umpteenth rainish day. Water from a branch drips slow and hits my cheek as I run, quick and cold like thinking about something suddenly. Alec.

. .

I prep myself. You're not supposed to ask. You're supposed to plan it out. I walk up and tell her. —Valentine's Day.

She wrinkles up. —Oh, Cole, do we have to? Could you just come over and we'll roll around or something? What are you doing? You're on the ground.

—I'm thanking the universe for the perfect girlfriend.

. .

We snap out of it together, a warm drooly doze in her room. She reaches up and slides the window shut, very beautiful. Right there, on her arm, the sort of beautiful spot like what made pioneers think, let's put a town here.

—I want to tell you something important.

My stomach dips into an *uh-oh*. I try to keep my eyes, my whole mind, just on the angle of skin across sky in my view of her arm and the window. Finally: —What is it?

It's a soft sigh she sighs, but substantial. —I just wish I had something, more or important, to say. Sometimes, you know? After the sex it's just nothing in my head with you.

Her arm moves and the sky is all I can see. But I have to say something. —A good nothing?

—Yeah.

If I moved my head maybe I could read it better, see where I am and where this is going. But it's so calm in my eyes, the blue so vacant, for once not a cloud in the sky. A good nothing.

· ·

—What does it taste like?

We're talking in the dark, a lot lately, easier and sexy.

—You know what it tastes like, Cole. Your body squirts it out all the time and you can't tell me you haven't been curious.

I decide not to think about Alec.

· ·

Her mom had a tea going, some sweet flowers she got sent from a town with a market in wherever they used to live. Rosy but not roses, some old wives' remedy tonic, poured into a jar with a tight metal lid to carry with you.

—Can I have some too?

Grisaille laughed. —It's for cramps.

—It smells good, though.

—Well, sure. I mean, it'll definitely work on *you.*

We sat on the drizzly steps a bit and I listened to her through a gossipy tangle she was having with two friends miles away onscreen. The steam steamed. The taste made my stomach noisy. I did not in fact have cramps all afternoon. She kicked her flats off talking, bare feet getting dirty and cute in the mess of leaves and weeds unmowed. Something stupid was on in the living room, and maybe it was the tea mixture, but we fell deep truly asleep for an hour and woke up in magic dusky light when it was over. We'd both dreamed something we couldn't remember all of, and we got giggly over how boring it was to hear the other one's dumb drony dream summary, all the spacey sentences reaching toward nothing. We made up better endings.

Her mom came back home, ravioli with butter, red wine with *don't tell your mother, Cole.* Grisaille's sleepy face, one kiss on the mouth and a pat on the hair, not sorry to go, just sorry to see it over. So, that day. That was as good as fucking, for sure I guess.

· ·

Halfway through the movie, Grisaille says it's boring. We make out a little and lose the thread of the plot. She pulls her jeans down, underwear, but keeps them around her ankles, lifts her legs up so my head just fits. I do my new trick of holding her ass, pressing her against my mouth when she comes, until she can't stand it and almost kicks me away. She says no when I unbuckle for my turn. —That wore me out. You can do it yourself and I'll watch you.

I do it quick, my mouth full of her and my chin sticky like I'm done with a peach. Did this with other girls but it was a show, slow to let them see. Here I just do it, come hard into my own hand grunting like it's happening, which it is, for real.

You're making me, Grisaille, into myself with you.

· ·

OK, we tried it, and now we know. It's not a good way to have sex. And also it's a bad way to eat hummus.

· ·

We have lunch, real lunch in a restaurant, and I tell her I love her. She doesn't talk for a bit. The waiter already hates us; she ordered red wine forgetting we weren't in Europe. I think some other guy, maybe at some European place with a bottle of wine between them, must have said it to her better.

—I don't know, Cole. I think you have said this to a lot of girls.

—I mean it.

—I know. That's what I mean. Every time, don't you, Cole, you mean it.

· ·

The songs where they say *you drive me crazy* I'm finally really getting. Her hips rising on the floor and her hands so busy there.

—Wait. No.

—I can't stay on my knees like this. She keeps pulsing.

—This one isn't. For you. Cole.

. .

My head in her armpit almost, half asleep, looking at the hairs there and when I inhale the smell for a second I think I'm with Alec and startle straight up like a nightmare.

—What?

—Nothing,

And I shake, make something up. —Foot fell asleep.

. .

That was a very short game of Truth or Dare we just did.

. .

She is laughing. My face is buried in her. It's not tickling and it's not eating her out. It's a thing I am inventing, so happy, talking right to her beautiful cunt. Goddamn delicious, I say, or something, out loud. C'mon juicy, so wet I love you, love everything, pucker up inside fuck.

—What are you even saying, crazy?

—Stay with me. Let's keep at it. Tastes so good.

. .

She asks it again, after I say I didn't hear her. —Would you do something with a guy?

—No.

—For me?

—Like, it turns you on? I don't know. Depends on what, depends on guy.

—Let me think.

—No, the answer is no.

. .

—Did you ever do anything with a girl?

—Last year my boyfriend was into that. He invited over this friend of his cousin. The cousin had this crazy motorcycle and was so fucking hot, Cole.

—Could you? Talk about the girl, or, maybe let's not talk about it.

. .

—It's OK, you look at other girls,

My eyes blush back to her. It was just she was climbing onto a bicycle, the crotch of her little pants just for a moment, every fold like the fold of her skin, climbing on.

Grisaille is smiling, though.

—but maybe, Cole, not when I am actually talking to you.

. .

—You know that girl Jana? She draws amazing.

—Yeah, I know her.

—*Amazing.* She was showing me about shading. See, look at the coffee cup. Wait. This one. I'm pretty proud of it. She showed me, see, how to make it, like down here, so the shadow kind of rounds it out.

—Wow.

I never thought of her like that. Grisaille looks at me, guesses it out.

—Her, too?

—We didn't, it was just one night at a party. We didn't sleep together.

—But you tried?

—I don't know. It didn't happen.

She shut the sketchbook and put her hands down on it.

—She draws *really*, really well.

—I didn't even know you then.

—I know, Cole. I was just hoping there was some-one who, I could find someone you haven't messed with.

I told Grisaille again that I didn't even know her then. And, did not add: still feel like that sometimes.

. .

She's on her stomach with her hands stretched out in front of her. I'm putting my clothes on. Her armpits, hairy, and her skin all the way down, is actually making me ache, an actual ache. She turns her head and her eyes are wet. Shit, crying?

—What's wrong?

—Nothing.

—What's,

—*Nothing.*

She says something in another language, I don't even know which one. She watches me not get it. —It's an expression. Who can I complain to, if I don't like the shape of the globe?

—Are you, did I,

She's almost disgusted at me. —It's not *you*, Cole. Everything in my head isn't what *you* do. I just miss him.

—Him who?
—*Them. Them. Everybody.*

. .

Maybe it's the town and everything, everyone in it. I'm not Portugal, nothing around here is Portugal. I run the longer trail, frowning at the puzzle of it, that I might be the apple or something of her eye, but that she is the whole horizon, everything I can look at and see.

Onscreen like always she's —Sorry about before.

—OK.

—Really. I think I'm getting sick is all.

I give her a smile but the stretch, the gap, the bridge that falls through sometimes even when it's built back up. We built it, everything almost we have, from sex, all the dirty parts are almost all the parts. It feels like enough when we're having it. But there are other times too. I can only pin her down, it scares me to realize I think this, when I'm pinning her down.

. .

Three days Grisaille's out. I feel like I'm on false legs, trying to laugh around with people I haven't really paid attention to lately. Lost and leashless. Alec won't even tell me to fuck off. Run longer. Actually ace a quiz. Draw something, badly at first and then maybe not so terrible, a piece of paper I then fold up for no reason and then, again, alone at the screen, too early for sleep, hello girls.

. .

Here they are near a swimming pool, in neighboring chairs that tilt way back. Her fingernails look too long to feel good inside her but she has two of them deep. The tans are ridiculous so I don't know why it works. Her nipples, the angle of her legs on his shoulders. I don't think of how uncomfortable it would be on those chairs. I think of Grisaille's chest, and how good it feels to come on her.

. .

Lots of babysitter ones. So many that everyone's dad must have watched one at least. Alana used to babysit a lot.

. .

—That's nuts. All the guys she's been with, she needs the friends she can get.

Her eyes do it again. —This is what I mean, Cole.

. .

I have a who-knows-where thought on a run, that I wish Alec could watch us. Just in a corner of the room. His cock in his hands. But when I think about looking at his face, I can't go on, and sprint it, fast fast faster until I'm panting too hard to even have it in my head anymore.

. .

—OK I did some gay stuff but I don't feel gay about it.

—Tell me what stuff.

—OK but don't tell anyone.

—Well I'm a guy on a random anonymous chat. I think you're safe.

. .

She is having her period again. It is true, a true thing obviously I cannot mention. Another true thing is, she

Grisaille's back coming through the door. I don't like how nervous I am about it, how wide I can feel my grin after the kiss is over. Her teeth are hungry on mine. —I really, *really* really missed you.

It is Grisaille saying this. I am embarrassed that I am grateful.

. .

—My mom's got it now, what I had. She's sick.

—That sucks.

—For us, yeah. Where can we go, where is there?

. .

Well, I haven't had an orgasm by these bleachers for a while.

. .

Compare and contrast the two treaties of Bucharest and finally getting to fuck in a bed again with your girlfriend tonight. Give examples. Give us the details.

. .

She is scooting over me, breathing odd, in the position girls usually do to dollop their breasts in your
mouth one by one. But she keeps on, her chest passing
by with a warm slide of the skin, until she drops her
belly onto my mouth. It's salty on my tongue, smooth
and gurgly. She is laughing now. —Eat my belly! Behold
it! Worship the belly!

I realize what it is, the salt I'm tasting, but I go crazy
on it anyway until she's yelping, shimmying, each *eek* a
super delight.

. .

—Give me a hint.
—Rhymes with funalingus.

. .

Her hands on my ass pushing me deeper and for a
second Alec is there in my head, in my cock.

—You came quick when I did that.

She's watching me, blinking. I pretend, to kill the
moment, I'm taking a bow.

. .

—There's my beautiful wife.

The guy's in the lobby of the mu
waiting outside the ladies room. He'
wife, I take it, means they're still fucl

. .

—Do you want to go to Greta's?

She yawns a little. —Whatever. I'n
—I know.

Her eyes go dark right quick. —
ever. You're pretty easy yourself, but
it, yes?

—Yes. They say I have a rep.

—For a boy, that's like a medal. Or
even if you don't like it, it's just som
For girls, it's like, she's a ruin, stay awa

—It's not like that. People get mad
I've been with, their friends, it's like a

—Not the same. You know Allison?
course you do. She won't talk to me l
next to each other in *three classes*, bec
we're fucking.

Grisaille's back coming through the door. I don't like how nervous I am about it, how wide I can feel my grin after the kiss is over. Her teeth are hungry on mine.

—I really, *really* really missed you.

It is Grisaille saying this. I am embarrassed that I am grateful.

. .

—My mom's got it now, what I had. She's sick.

—That sucks.

—For us, yeah. Where can we go, where is there?

. .

Well, I haven't had an orgasm by these bleachers for a while.

. .

Compare and contrast the two treaties of Bucharest and finally getting to fuck in a bed again with your girlfriend tonight. Give examples. Give us the details.

. .

She is scooting over me, breathing odd, in the position girls usually do to dollop their breasts in your mouth one by one. But she keeps on, her chest passing by with a warm slide of the skin, until she drops her belly onto my mouth. It's salty on my tongue, smooth and gurgly. She is laughing now. —Eat my belly! Behold it! Worship the belly!

I realize what it is, the salt I'm tasting, but I go crazy on it anyway until she's yelping, shimmying, each *eek* a super delight.

. .

—Give me a hint.

—Rhymes with funalingus.

. .

Her hands on my ass pushing me deeper and for a second Alec is there in my head, in my cock.

—You came quick when I did that.

She's watching me, blinking. I pretend, to kill the moment, I'm taking a bow.

· ·

—There's my beautiful wife.

The guy's in the lobby of the multiplex. We're both waiting outside the ladies room. He's old, but *beautiful wife*, I take it, means they're still fucking.

· ·

—Do you want to go to Greta's?

She yawns a little. —Whatever. I'm easy.

—I know.

Her eyes go dark right quick. —I mean it. Don't ever. You're pretty easy yourself, but I bet nobody says it, yes?

—Yes. They say I have a rep.

—For a boy, that's like a medal. Or maybe a hat, like even if you don't like it, it's just something he wears. For girls, it's like, she's a ruin, stay away from her.

—It's not like that. People get mad at me too. Girls I've been with, their friends, it's like a minefield.

—Not the same. You know Allison? Never mind, of course you do. She won't talk to me hardly, and we're next to each other in *three classes*, because she knows we're fucking.

—That's nuts. All the guys she's been with, she needs all the friends she can get.

Her eyes do it again. —This is what I mean, Cole.

. .

I have a who-knows-where thought on a run, that I wish Alec could watch us. Just in a corner of the room. His cock in his hands. But when I think about looking at his face, I can't go on, and sprint it, fast fast faster until I'm panting too hard to even have it in my head anymore.

. .

—OK I did some gay stuff but I don't feel gay about it.

—Tell me what stuff.

—OK but don't tell anyone.

—Well I'm a guy on a random anonymous chat. Think you're safe.

. .

She is having her period again. It is true, a true thing obviously I cannot mention. Another true thing is, she is crying very hard over an orange she unpeeled and it turned out to be moldy. I'm walking around her like a hummingbird until she makes me sit down. She tries to laugh, and cries harder. She tries to say something, and hiccups in the middle; I lean in to try to hear whatever it is her mouth is saying. She kisses me instead, her lips sloppy from weeping, hiccupy again but her hands are already running down my body. I'm in her before my shirt is off, my socks on my feet against her socks on her feet. She bites my shoulder and tears a rip I'll always see. But no one else will.

. .

So, with Alec, I give up, I guess. How long with typing to him without answer, before I don't even think to do it? What's there to say about it except, I'm straight and I like girls, and it was just whatever it was?

Keep finding porn he would like, and can't send it to him.

. .

On the floor I see some drawings she half-made, a couple flowers, some guy's chin over and over, stubbly, the windowsill so clear for a minute it looks like a photo. She's not even taking a class, and me with my assigned sketchbook I don't even know where it is. The chin is mine, I realize, I think, I think.

. .

I'm telling you she started it, a whisper one night with both hands on me up and down.

—Would you fuck another girl?

I could do nothing but pretend not to hear her.

—Tell me.

But I was already harder in her hands. She climbed up with a long kiss, moving her hips, the tip of my cock just barely inside her. —Would you—

—Stop.

—fuck another girl?

—*Yes.*

She plunged onto me. —A first-year.

—What?

—You know, at school. Do you look at them?

—We don't call them first-years.

—Do you? You do look at them.

I leaned up to bite her shoulder a little but she growled away. —I know you look at them all the time. *Wait.*

Her hands pressed my shoulders back down and she made it slow. —I want you to.

—What?

—Tonight, tonight. I want you to find a girl at this party, and fuck her.

—*Jesus.*

She climbed off me and I had trembles like never before. Her eyes looked like a demon in a poster. She locked in to stare at me, her hand quick down her body and busy between her legs.

—You're crazy.

—Find her . . .

She said it over the sound of it, in and out of her own self. —Find her, Cole and, no, I will pick her out.

—Grisaille!

—and *fuck her.*

I came with nobody touching me, a wet firework in the air. I heard it patter down on us and she came too. We said nothing for the rest of the song fading out.

—Were you serious?

She wouldn't look at me. —*Yes.*

—What is this?

—It's just something I want, Cole. It—

—It turns you on?

—It turns me on so much.

And her hand was already on me again and I was fierce and striving with it. —You're so hard. I *love* your cock hard, Cole.

But she peeled off me and stood shouldering into her bra, the sunset in the window blazing a ragey scarlet behind her back. It was still early, but the way we were talking about it, felt already too late.

—Come back.

—No. I want to save it. I want you to save it for *her*.

I rolled the other way and saw an empty bottle on her desk, the usual Spanish or something wine they had cases of. But did she open it tonight, was my question now. Did she finish it alone. —I *really* want this, Cole.

—This is fucked up.

She was in the mirror with lipstick. Her hair was tousled, untamed. It looked fucked, like we'd been fucking.
—There's nothing fucked up about it. They look at you, Cole, they want something. Give it to them.

—Are you really serious?

—Get dressed. I'll open a wine.

· ·

It was glaring busy inside the party. Kristen, not a lot of people I knew. Grisaille raised her eyes at some girl with braids and another, with her friend, dancing over-wild to a song not cool enough for the rest of every-body. And then nervous on a couch, blonde and her eyes painted girly with too much care, too excited for the party, looking around with a big red plastic cup of something, her cheeks flushing, that she'd probably never had before. Grisaille was in my ear with it, licking and whispering. She went to fix three gin and tonics, limes bobbing and sliced too big, so strong the music warbled just with the first sip. —I wish I could watch.

She was slurring like a creature, but we are creatures. The teacher said it in Art, *we are creatures,* a big wild painting of sinners and punishments with everyone looking like an animal. Monsters sometimes. I felt my smile start up as I walked toward her, crawling up my face like fish hooks were doing it. But it was me. I did it. I did her. There is no way, I cannot between ravage and tonic forget the details.

—Hey.

—Hi.

She was grateful not to be alone. But I just asked if there was room on the couch, and, —What's your name? I'm Cole.

—Yeah, everybody knows you.

—I have a rep, I guess.

She laughed at how I shrugged off how dangerous she knew me to be. She was nice, she was smiling, *Courtney* she was almost shouting in my ear over the speakers near us on the mantel. Some talk about a thing onscreen everyone's sharing. Move my arm round. Move her arm around. Legs rubbing a little by accident, on purpose. Courtney biting her lip and spoiling her makeup.

Upstairs, it was some little girl's room. Cartoon sheets. The kiss was sweet and fluttery, so wrong for what I was doing. She held my head to kiss me more, it felt like a skull. She unbuttoned her own shirt, with help, slipped down her pants with a silky scarf she'd rigged as a belt. Her eyes were shiny and flat, though, glassy like in old museum tableaus. Endangered species. Another kiss that was nothing but gin and spit, and her hands, both of them, between my legs too rough but not too rough not to work. My pants locked chain-gang around my ankles, so I stopped. To kick off my shoes, I stopped. My hand already had the condom Grisaille had found and put in my pocket, but it still felt like there was something up for grabs, a shaky question in the air. She was sitting up a little, to kiss me again or maybe to leave, a fierce kiss on the mouth.

—Do you want to?

And then,

—Are we good?

is what I muttered against her, and she nodded and nodded, fast like chattering teeth. And then her grunts, harsh, and my name, *Cole*, but no other words, not *stop*, not anything. A tight fuck quick. Definitely not *no*, neither of us said that. Our mouths kept busy doing anything but *no*. These details scraping at me, telling not even myself what happened, and with *are you OK?* and *Yeah OK* I was back in the hallway, downstairs with my shoes still untied. Grisaille was very drunk, alone on a folding chair they'd backed into a corner, almost passed out.

—You smell like her.

—Let's go home.

Her kiss was fast, very ferocious. —You are so fucking hot, you make me almost—

I didn't like my voice. —Let's. Go. Home.

The street was filthy, after a storm. My mind smelled of it. I had not, exactly, agreed exactly to do this, but now, wasn't it, it was done. Neither of us got sick, not enough drunk even to be sick in our homes when we separated to stumble the rest of the way. But we were, weren't we, sick, both of us, sick creatures with our tricks.

Courtney, I thought, unshowered in bed, sticky and too quivery inside to sleep. Sickened the most by Grisaille's murmur in my ear, as slippery as the rest of her all night, *next time it's mine. The next turn,* such a terrible whisper, *belongs to me.* I felt blacked out but I didn't black out. I know every detail, I'm sorry, forever with every other dirty thing rolled up and riled in my brain and cock. *Are we good?* Just because I'm not listing it, just because— Alec in my head—I'm not telling every detail, doesn't mean I wasn't there thrilled and queasy fucking her for all of it.

· ·

So, thirteen now, is the number.

· ·

—Can we talk about it?
—What part?
I make my fingers stop twitching over the keys. The part I didn't like, I want to tell her. The part making me pace around with loud music. But I just ask if I can come over and I run there sweaty and hard to do it quick leaving me still thirsty, or something. Rattly. Sad. What rope can you lower to get me out of here?

. .

—And if I fucked another boy?

She's still straddling me. In a second my cock will wilt up and slip out of her like a water balloon. —What other boy are we talking about?

She laughs. We drop it. Thank God.

. .

—Is something bothering you?

This is my mother saying this. I slam off. —Yes.

. .

It's like drinking, I want to tell someone. I am running because there's no one to tell. You drink too much sometimes, learning to do it right, the way you want. Courtney, it's the same with how you learn to fuck. Until you figure it out, you're going to be sick some mornings.

. .

—It's not fair, Cole, but OK.

—I just didn't like it.

The window rattles. It's late. —But you fucked her anyway, right? So why can't—

—You can't. I don't. Please don't. Please won't you— and I'm quiet but still saying it out loud in my skull. I knew, I told myself and I told myself. *I knew you weren't safe.*

· ·

Like lightning in my spine it's that sudden. I'm mid-sentence in the overflowing kitchen.

—What?

I shake my head, gesture to Jeremy like a wall fell down in front of my face. My beer tastes strange, bad, and I move sweaty, like I already know it. I don't even ask anyone as I scowl around the living room, but Alec's eyes are on me, very black, very bright. I think later he must have known right then, but right then I tell myself I don't know anything. Up the stairs and the landing and the other stairs. Fling open one wrong door, the bathroom, the closet, door after door, too stupid and too frantic. I don't like the sounds I'm either hearing or making. And the stripe of light rectangles onto Grisaille

on the older brother's bed. Jack has his pants off and
she's kissing his neck until they turn around to face me.
Her face is a bright, a little sweaty, a little shame. But
her hand doesn't move from around his thick cock.

. .

—I thought it was sexy.
—*Yeah*, obviously.
—Cole. Like a game. Like with the first-year.
My voice is so spitty I hate it myself. —We don't
even call it that in America.
—*Cole*.
—
—Cole. I'm leaving anyway. At the end of the
semester.
I'm choking something up. —Did he feel better
than me?
—How do I know how he felt?
—Was it better?
She kicks the ground. Her hands are clenched and
I can't stop seeing them around his cock. Bigger than
mine. —I just thought it was fun.

. .

She had her hand on another guy's cock, I have a sick zigzag in my head of it like I'm typing it all out. To be honest, I keep typing, it turns me on sometimes, a flicker in my ankles and my mouth, churned up thinking about the details, disgusted and cold and erect. I'm not typing this to anyone, there's no one to do it to. I'm not even typing it out loud.

· ·

Raging awake, pacing so loud my mom makes sure I'm OK. Sure, I'm OK. Her hand around his cock like that. Try to come, just to get some sleep, but every cock on the screen is his. Watch the girl-to-girl stuff, gets it done.

· ·

—End of the semester I'm leaving, so,
—Stop saying that. You don't get to fuck people over just because you used to live in Cairo and then pack up and get on a plane.
—Make this quick, Cole. Can you get over this?
I'm letting her cup my face. I can feel my cheeks squinting furious. *Are we good,* is what she's asking.

—Can we just have a few more weeks having fun and—

—You were jacking him off.

· ·

I wish anything, *anything* was hacking at me except for this. Feeling stupid and not smart enough to stop it. A teacher is repeating himself and still I do not, will not fucking listen to what it is he is saying, I can only hear what is getting at me. A *girl*, I want to tell him, a *girl-friend*, surely even this lousy ugly man knows the drill of how much it is drilling in me, and will leave me alone while I shiver it out at my desk.

· ·

—You were fucking jacking him off.

—I'm not, I'm not going to deny it or something.

—*My* girlfriend!

—Remember, Cole, we said it could be *anything*. We said, we both did, that we could call it—

—You're my *girlfriend*, that's what it's called, that's what *anybody* would call it—

—Yes but then, but the other night,

—I didn't give you permission.

—*Permission?*

She is furious behind her glasses, the glare of the streetlight. In the mirror that time, naked except for those glasses blinking and fucking. Her hand on his cock back at the party.

—*Permission?*

. .

There's cheating, I say on a run alone and cold, and there's sleeping with a lot of people. There's another girl at a party when I go along with it, and another guy at a party when I don't. I am, it's like, glaring at two equations on a blackboard having their different operations pointed out when I do not fucking care about either, any of them.

. .

We are monsters with it. Told you, told you. I am saying this to myself. *Are we good,* no we are fucking not.

. .

Another, though, to deal with that river-god of the blood: hidden, guilty.

. .

—Don't say that, Cole. Take it back right now or, don't you dare,
—*Slut.*
—*Fuck you! You?* You with every girl you have been inside all over this school warning me. And you say,
—It's different.
—Cole, you know what *slut* is? There isn't one for boy. It's a punishing, it's a fucked-up word for a girl, *only*, who likes sex. There's no guy word for it.
—*Guy.* Is the word.

. .

—Don't talk to me.
—You mean now or like ever?
—
—Grisaille did you get my last message?
—
—OK just say if you got it.
—

. .

Robin knows. Gus knows. Janie knows. Word spreads, it's in the air like something I can't breathe.

. .

Find another girl and fuck her to get over it, says some new terrible buddy in my head. The only one I can think of is the first-year and how nervous she was, scared. *First-year,* now you're doing it.

. .

I am heaving, sitting on the edge of the tub fully dressed. Heaving with how much I want her, and how the shame sickens me. She's the only one I would let see me like this.

. .

You know her name's not even a real name, Cole. You know it's some art technique or whatever.

. .

I'm searching for a clip I can see in my head, hot and
filthy, hard in my underwear on the bed leaning over on
the screen looking for it, when it hits me thunderously
and I wilt and almost, sort of, vomit. It's just one night
with Grisaille in her bed, not porn. Never find that no
matter how you search on your screens, you stupid broken fuck.

· ·

The trouble, I realized buying myself an awful, idiotic
soda or something, standing with it cold in my hand
outside the store. Girl in a car laughing at something
the guy said in sunglasses. I tried to show you the real
person I am. I let that happen when it seemed like the
coast was clear. But the real me is terrible. You saw I am
an asshole. But you, your hands I miss so much, you
got away from me. And I'm stuck here. Yes, that is the
trouble. You've figured it out, moron with a can in your
hands, alone, congratulations.

· ·

The party rumbles and me quiet for hours, who
knows what I say to who knows who I'm talking to.

Beer in my hand and then it's empty, fourth time. Some freeze-over maybe when I say something, or did I just glare and everyone left the room, shaky in my eyes, on the sofa shaking and trying to talk to Alec who has stayed there, out of habit, out of loyalty, or maybe he's just too scared to go. I can only say it once, that I miss him so fucking much.

· ·

Driving around not as late as it feels. Too early to go home. Music no help, the seatbelt the only thing in the world that wants to hold me. There used to be *places*. Things kept me out at night. By *things* I mean you, Grisaille, answer something will you? Fuck me for old time's sake, just give me your voice on the phone, your name on the little screen. Stupid lonely Friday. Saturday and Sunday ahead like a cliff.

· ·

Who can I complain to, if I don't like the shape of the globe?

· ·

We're all happy, I tell myself. She's gliding someplace tonight like she does, she should be happy. Alec's
around someplace making it work. And I have everything I could, a clear night in this corner of a parking
lot smelling like dogs. Happy, fuck it, it's not working.

· ·

—Your father and I are going to try that new Thai
restaurant, Cole, if you want to come with us.

Wondering if they serve poison there.

· ·

I think I see her holding hands with a guy and my
blood froths up in my head until it is revealed he is a
grown man pushing a shopping cart, because it is a gro-
cery store and she's not here.

Grisaille. You have corrupted my imagination.

· ·

It's a Boy, says a row of balloons in a window, down
the block. Poor thing, I think, on the other side of the
car window. Too late for you.

. .

This morning, Cole, you decided to focus on your run. But you seem to be sidetracked, or anyway are focused on this tree you are leaning on, breathing and crying on it.

. .

C'mon, I am saying silently. I am saying it in the field we went to. My throat hurts so maybe it is getting shouted after all. C'mon! C'mon! I don't even know the rest of it.

. .

I miss her, I'm coaching at myself as I trudge toward school, like I missed a bus. Not like a limb, a life, an everything.

. .

Had that coming, is the national opinion I guess at school. With my rep. Surprised nobody castrated that dude, somebody or everybody is saying.

. .

This is not, while I am standing here, happiness. It is not half-happiness. It is so far from any happiness I have had once, that the light from that happiness is taking years and years to reach me here trying not to cry in this stupid class I'm in.

. .

Stolen is how it feels, looking around the yard wondering what bench to disappear into. I know she's not a possession I owned, but still I can't help it. She was *in* my possession. In my arms, at least. In your legs, it sounds dirty I know but I miss it. Sex with you, in you, the dirtiest parts and all of it, too, the rest, the whole thing gone like it was taken.

. .

A year later, and I'm fine. I've learned my lesson, my comeuppance, I've zipped up and treated everyone right. I'm making this up, desperately. I'm happy now. A year later and the clock on the wall in the school in the middle of my endless painful day has not moved two minutes.

. .

The first-year even meets my eyes with a little sad shrug before I can say sorry, or whatever it was I was going to say when I stopped in the crowded doorway. My rep, who doesn't know about it. Courtney can't be surprised. She knew, she tells herself, what she was getting in for.

. .

So this week I have this other guy I know, Oliver, hanging out a little. He's the nicest person, the only one right now being nice. But what am I going to tell him?

. .

Kristen leans over so her head is level with mine, flat on the desk. Her boyfriend, it's been how long and she's still so happy with him, is waiting in the doorway.

—Whatever happened, you totally deserve it and it's totally your fault.

I tell her I know.

—But I do pity you, if that helps.

I have to say something. —You know what would help?

But she's already walked away.

· ·

In the shower the water feels like her mouth everywhere. Get hard, get lonely, the patheticness, dude, of your wretched life this morning. These are the details, somebody. And every night I fall wide-awake on my mattress.

· ·

I wasn't just a fuck to them, any of them probably, is what I'm seeing. For every girl I thought I was uncomplicated sex, it wasn't. Put it this way: if you can't see the complication, you're probably it. I zipped up in all those places, left them walking out of my car, or a kiss at the bus stop. And they shivered like this, while I did nothing but lick my lips, thrust through all of it. And then to Alec.

· ·

I sit down on a bench next to this girl from Bio last year.

—I'm having a shitty day.

But she just puts her bag on her shoulder right away.

—I have a boyfriend, Cole.

. .

The nighttime's closing in like the same trap, definitely time to go home and jump out of my skin. In my room stalking around with my shoes off, flopping down to roll and reroll on my bed. Stupid and stupefied, my eyes on the ceiling, the wrecked-up blanket, wide open. And every time I shut them it's that place by the open elbow, comfortable and safe as she reaches over us to slide shut the window. That spot right there, front and center forever in my goddamn head it won't stop.

. .

It's one thing to write love poems. Another, though,
to deal with that river-god of the blood: hidden, guilty.
Even the girl, who thinks she knows her young lover,
even she isn't close enough for him to tell
how this lord of lust—in the lonely times

before she knew him, before she eased him, almost
before she seemed possible—would lift up his cock,
wet with the unknowable, and churn the night
to an endless riot.

. .

I read it nineteen times or maybe once, when I see what it is. I haven't been able to get to her in forever, I'm blocked, but she sent it to me blindly, I see. Blind-copied when she sends it to some address, her old teacher maybe, in Germany. But she couldn't send it if I was still blocked, right? Even though I'm blocked now, trying for the fifth time, just blank with *please* in the subject, it means sometime she turned it off. She unblocked it even for just a minute, for just a minute maybe she wouldn't have minded hearing from me.

Is that what it means? Or is it just, Look, I put *cock* in the poem after all?

. .

After some dance, the something alliance, Alec has a *boyfriend* for a little while. I hear this.

I start to tell him. —I heard that—

—It's true.

He stops walking in the hallway. His shoulders, I don't know, relax a little. I think of them bare, trembling from somewhere. It's a very tiny smile on his face.

—Is he cool?

—You know, I thought about getting a cool one, but then I just chose a big douche.

—Ha. OK. Sorry. I'm sure he's awesome. I hope,

—You hope what?

—I don't know, what's he, I don't know, what's he like?

Alec looks at me like a dog in from the mud. *What are we going to do with you, boy?* —Bi.

It takes me a minute to figure out he means bisexual and not see-you-later. He's laughing and we both, a little, laugh.

I don't even know what I'm even asking. —Do you want to—

But he's down the hall and then it's just a few words every so often for the rest of the year.

. .

—No, no.

He's shaking his head professionally, the guidance

counselor. I have brochures in my hand from all the finagling I've done. Opportunities abroad.

—What?

—If she's leaving we haven't heard. She just turned in her registration papers, late I might add. Grisaille Avelar is enrolled for next year.

. .

—When you are older—

That's the only part of the advice I hear. But, Dad, I'm not.

. .

The screen shows me Portugal. The screen shows me Cairo. They have a thing where you can wander the streets. I can go anywhere I want is what the screen keeps telling me. Try this. Try there. Go around here. The world's wide open. You can wander anyplace and you'll be alone there, too.

. .

So, what is it? Time to go home, but I *am*. Late, late, all the music seems tired. Sparky inside my body but no one will have me, no one I can find or want to possess. Strip down in my room, the weather warming, tip tap on the screen, hello girls. But it fails. Nothing moves me. My hands on my knees, my face so tired in its screened reflection. Who is it, hello, what girl, who's out there someplace to jolt me happy, to color the world sexy again? Grisaille has thieved them all away from me, all these naked girls look just like her. Wishing I could watch every beautiful fuck with her, just to breathe it a little. Wish I could bring up all my time with her, Grisaille and start it, whatever the words, that lead to the flesh and the warm and the happy in bed. I'm hard with it. My mouth's hungry thinking of her wet, but it's dry trying to think what to say. I rattle my fingers on the buttons, wondering what buttons to push. Grisaille, Grisaille. Naked. Every girl I can see, their voices, so sad delicious, all sound like her, the only girl I can call up is Grisaille. I do it, trembling broken and so hard. Hello? Help me, hello?

· ·

—Hello?

(RIP Prince)

A NOTE ON THE AUTHOR

DANIEL HANDLER is the author of the novels *We Are Pirates*, *The Basic Eight*, *Watch Your Mouth*, *Adverbs*, and *Why We Broke Up*, a 2012 Michael L. Printz Honor Book. As Lemony Snicket, he is responsible for many books for children, including the thirteen-volume sequence *A Series of Unfortunate Events* and the four-book series *All the Wrong Questions*. He is married to the illustrator Lisa Brown and lives with her and their son in San Francisco.